Baker's Hawk

Jack Bickham

Baker's Hawk

Doubleday & Company, Inc.
Garden City, New York, 1974

All the characters in this book
are fictitious, and any resemblance
to actual persons, living or dead,
is purely coincidental.

First Edition
ISBN: 0-385-05724-5 Trade
0-385-01852-5 Prebound
Library of Congress Catalog Card Number 73–79644
Copyright © 1974 by Jack M. Bickham
All Rights Reserved
Printed in the United States of America

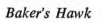

Baker's Hawk

One

Night was coming to the Oregon sky. To the west, over jagged peaks, pink clouds drifted against the cobalt horizon; to the east, the Cascades stood sawtooth black in a wine-colored infinity. There was a little road, yellow-dusty, which was visible only here and there as it twisted between hills.

A buggy drawn by a single horse came along the road, moving through a valley where it was hidden by upthrusting firs, then visible again as the road labored upward and the trees seemed to fall away on either side because of the steepness of the terrain. There were two men in the buggy: the driver, a bulky businessman of perhaps fifty, and a much younger man, also wearing a somber business suit, whip thin, with long blond hair.

The older man flicked the reins to speed the horse. "Getting chilly," he observed.

The younger man smiled and took a deep breath of the sweet, cool air. "It's a lot like home."

"Well, we ought to make it back to town in another thirty minutes or so. I guess we won't freeze by then, anyhow."

1

The younger man, William R. Baker, attorney-at-law, did not reply. He felt good: relaxed, very tired, and keen with anticipation. The trip to inspect the land had been tough, but the inspection had borne out all his expectations and then some. It was good, virgin land, heavily timbered and in an ideal location. His report to the investors in Denver would be affirmative.

Chumley, the older man, drove for a mile or two in silence. Baker knew the questions that the rancher wanted to ask; he allowed Chumley to figure out the best way to open the subject.

Finally, as they drove down the side of a hill toward another valley and woods below, Chumley came out with it directly.

"Well, Mister Baker, you've seen the parcel of land. What's your opinion?"

"I like it," Baker told him forthrightly.

"Good."

"I also think the price is a shade too high."

"Too high!"

"Yes sir."

"Say," Chumley growled, "with the way land speculation is going in this country these days, the price we're asking is dirt cheap!"

"Two hundred is high. The same sort of land east of Corvallis would go in the one-eighty range."

"That's east of Corvallis. We—"

"The Duggan land transaction in this area six months ago showed a price in the one-sixties."

Chumley glanced at him with new respect. "What do you know about the Duggan sale?"

Baker smiled at him. "Duggan, Brownson, and Plimmer, sale to Fredrickson, et al. Proposed January of 1894,

2

closed February of 1894. Papers registered February 16. Legal description—"

"All right, all right! You've done some homework."

"The people I represent do not want to be unreasonable, Mister Chumley. But yes, we do our homework."

Chumley clucked to the horse. He was not angry. He seemed to be enjoying the haggling. There was an impish admiration in his eyes as he gave Baker a sidelong glance. "Of course there was a cloud on the Duggan title."

"No more than on this property," Baker told him.

"There's no cloud on this land!"

Baker shrugged. "It's no problem, certainly. It's the usual kind of cloud for land in this area. It's certainly no major obstacle."

"You know that, do you," Chumley grunted.

"Yes," Baker said quietly.

"I suppose," Chumley blurted, "you've checked all that out too."

"Yes," Baker said again, just as quietly.

Chumley sighed. "Well, sir, I'll admit it: When I saw you get off that train, and I saw how young you were, and all, I thought, 'Well, Burt, old boy, you've got you a fresh chicken for the plucking.' I figured, first off, I'd walk and ride you into the ground today. I figured, second off, you wouldn't know a contract from a pine cone. *Now* I figure I better start looking at my hole card. I've got myself in a game with a real shark here!"

Baker grinned at him. "I'm no shark. I just want to represent my clients."

"I'd say your clients have got them a real lawyer."

It was a nice compliment, the kind that a man of Chumley's gruff character did not give unless it was meant. Baker paused, considering his reply, thinking he should mention

3

the meeting tomorrow afternoon with the other landhold-
ers, and that was when he saw the hawk.

He had seen a lot of hawks, and whether the sight of this
particular one was affecting because it was unexpected, or
because it was so beautiful, he had no way of knowing.

It struck him instantly, however, and deep—this particular hawk, alone, far off to the east, between his position
and the upvaulting face of a mountain: It was at first a
sweeping movement in the air at a great distance, and then
a high shaft of sunlight touched rust-colored wings, and
the hawk soared high, very high, with infinite grace, up
beyond the mountain backdrop into the wine sky. It soared,
and even at the distance Baker imagined he heard its lonely
cry.

Chumley saw his look. "Lots of hawks around here. I
suppose you got 'em in Colorado, too."

"Yes," Baker said. "I had a red-tailed hawk like that myself once, a long time ago."

"Is that a fact! You raise him, did you?"

"I—didn't quite finish."

"Well." Chumley was a little stumped. "Hawks are mighty
pretty. Of course, they can be a nuisance. They like to kill,
you know. They're loners, hawks are."

"That's just their nature," Baker said, and smiled because
he realized he was quoting from very old memory. "You
can never ask any being," he went on, repeating the pre-
cise words, "to change its nature."

"Well, now," Chumley muttered, and was flummoxed,
and fell silent.

The hawk circled in the sky and vanished.

The mood it had suddenly and inexplicably aroused in
Baker, however, was not so easy to put away. The coincidence of this particular kind of night, this particular location, and this particular red-tailed hawk had worked an

4

alchemy in his memory. The things that came back to him now were more vivid than they had been in a number of years. He was touched and saddened, and he said nothing.

Chumley, seeming to sense that the hawk had opened a door into something long ago, lapsed into quiet for the remainder of the ride back to the town.

When they arrived at the hotel, there was a brief conversation about tomorrow afternoon's conference. With a handshake, Chumley left him. Baker went into the hotel, had a light supper in the cafe, and went to his room.

Night lay over the country by this time, and the sky was alive with stars. Baker stood at the window of his hotel, looking down the narrow, dusty street of cabarets and stores and shacks, and past the big livery barn at the far end to the vastness of the mountain wilderness beyond.

You imagined old things were put away, he thought, and in one way they were indeed gone forever. But in another way the past was never behind a man; he carried it in his mind and sinew, and in his gut. And he never knew when it would come back.

It did no good to remember, he told himself. He was twenty-three years old; his new law practice was growing with his reputation and ability and nerve; he had everything going his way, and only a fool would look back to that time a dozen years ago when a skinny kid had had his entire life changed by a series of accidents.

But Baker was remembering. There was no help for it. He stood at his window and looked out on the Oregon night, and went back.

Two

The hawk was born on April 15, 1882, a few miles out from the small town of Springer, Colorado, on the western slope of the mountains. Actually there were three baby hawks hatched in the nest that day, but right from the start Billy Baker had his eye on just one of them.

The parent hawks had come back very early this year, first appearing in the distant sky while there was still snow in the valley where Billy lived with his parents. The snow had retreated up the mountainsides late in March, and Billy had spotted the hawks nesting high up in the vee of a juniper.

The tree chosen by the hawks was one Billy knew. Owls had nested there the year before, and he had figured out a way to climb a broken rock cliff quite nearby, to watch them from hiding. The hawks had picked out not only the same tree, but the same nest, rebuilding and enlarging it with twigs and brush, and lining the big, deep cavity with boughs from soft conifers. Billy had to attend school in Springer every day until early afternoon, and then there were farm chores to do. But nearly every afternoon, late, he hiked into the foothills to check his two beaver traps and sometimes to fish and almost always to check on the hawks. He knew when the rust-speckled eggs appeared in the nest, now as big as a baby cradle, and he knew about when the eggs would hatch, because he had asked around about such matters. He waited impatiently, and enjoyed watching the female guard her eggs while the male, hunting, swept far across the sky, often going out of vision.

The hawks were red-tails, big ones, with heavy bodies and wings that spread almost as far as Billy could stretch out his arms. They were a dark brownish-gray, with white breasts shading back to tan, and then to their flared red tails. When they flew, shades of tan and white and red and rust caught in the thin sunlight. They never seemed to make a bad move in the sky. They were just about the most beautiful things in the world. Billy never tired of watching them.

"What are you up to?" his father asked him one night at the supper table. They were at the plank table in front of the fireplace in their single-room house, just the three of them, quiet, and the question startled Billy.

"I'm not up to *anything*," he said guiltily.

His father gave him a stern look. He was a tall man, lank, with close-cropped dark hair and a stubble beard that made his jaws blue-black. He didn't ever smile much, although he was not cruel.

"You're up to something," his father said with certainty. "You've raced through feeding the chickens and forking in the barn every day for weeks now. You even helped make the soap without complaining. Then, the minute you're through every day, you light out for the tall timber. What have you got up there? Another coon?"

"No, I don't have another coon."

"I won't have you dragging another coon in here."

"I don't have my eye on one, honest."

7

Billy's mother, a pretty blond woman, younger, murmured, "He's doing all his work, Dan."

"I know that, Ellen. I just don't like the way he always slips off by himself. It ain't fitten'."

"I just like to fish, and stuff," Billy said.

"You're almost twelve, boy. You got to start growing up to be a man."

Billy's mother sort of sighed, "Oh, Dan."

"Well, Ellen, he has to learn."

"I know that. But he has time yet."

"We have to get the garden in. We have to paint. There's fence down. I'm not made of money. I need his help. He has to learn to stand on his own two feet and make his own way in the world soon."

Billy said, "I'll do what you say, Paw. Tell me. I'll do it."

His father's face screwed up as if he were in pain. "*I* know that, son. I'm not trying to badger you. I just want— you just have to *learn,* that's all!"

"Yes, sir."

His father looked at his mother. "School's out in another couple of weeks, and then we *have to* get at the plowing. For all I know, he's out roaming around the countryside when he ought to be doing his lessons!"

"I talked to Mrs. Reynolds just the other day," Billy's mother said calmly. "She says he's doing just fine."

Dan Baker threw up his hands. "All right! But no more coons around here, boy! I mean it! We've got rabbits out there, we've got that pet coon out there, we've got those stupid mice in those boxes out there, we've got Rex—for all the good the useless hound ever does—we've got all these blasted cats running around, and I'm not having any more! You're going to have to get rid of some of these pets. The next thing, you'll be trying to make pets of those fool chickens!"

8

It crossed Billy's mind to point out that he wasn't likely to make pets of the chickens; they were too stupid, for one thing, and he also liked to eat them too much. But that would have been very bad tactics, so all he said was, "Yes, sir."

It seemed to satisfy his father, and the rest of the meal passed in silence except when Mom told about the preacher coming by; Paw just snorted.

After the meal, Paw went out directly to get the milch cow in. Billy was still at the table, spooning out the last of the pudding. His mother leaned over him. She smiled, and her gold hair hung down so that the firelight behind it was crimson.

"Billy," she said softly.

"Yessum?"

"*Do* you have some new pet out there in the woods?"

"No, ma'am." Which was *true;* all he had so far were the eggs, at a distance at that.

She patted his head. "You're a good boy."

It sounded nice enough, but he knew better. He was a liar, if not in fact then in intent, and his plan was going to get him into a whole lot of trouble—unless he was awfully careful.

He figured he might—just *might,* it wasn't all that definite—get himself a hawk. After all, there were three eggs in the nest, and he might be able to climb up and get one of the babies if they hatched out.

He told himself he *might* do that.

But when the eggs hatched, and the baby hawks appeared in the nest, he knew he was probably a goner. That was because, right from the start, this one hawk—the one he knew he wanted—was different from the other two.

They all hatched pretty much alike, naked, awkward,

9

slippery little things with stubs where their wings should have been and soft little beaks surmounting gaping mouths that looked as big as doughnut holes. One of the three, though—Billy's—was slightly smaller. Billy noticed this immediately. He also learned, on later days, that the parents fed whichever baby put up the biggest struggle to get the food and made the most noise. The mother or father would come back to the nest, a dark knife-slash against the evening sky, and bring prey: a small bird, sometimes a field mouse, other times fat grubs or other insects. *Plop*. The food went into the mouth that yelled the loudest and fought hardest to outreach its competitors. Baker's hawk—that was the way Billy was thinking of it already—was not quite as pushy as the other two. Sometimes he didn't get fed at all. He moved around in the nest and got some food, but not as much as the other two, and they grew somewhat faster than he did because of it.

By the time school was let out for the summer, the baby hawks were covered with puffy soft down, and their feathers had begun to develop. They climbed up onto the lip of the nest often now and looked around and flapped their developing wings, making a great racket but getting nowhere. They were half the size of their parents one weekend when Billy observed them, and then he was busy for several days, helping his father get the corn and squash planted, and when he got back to the cliff hiding place to observe again, the babies seemed to have grown much larger, as if by magic.

Before long, they were going to fly.

That would be the turning point. Billy knew this. Once the young hawks were flying, it would probably be beyond his ability to catch one of them. He knew that he ought to try to climb the tree now and get one of the babies—*his* hawk—if he was going to do so.

10

It would not have been that difficult. The parents often were gone for long periods of time now, leaving the three fat, developing young hawks on their own. There were enemies around: Crows abounded in the area, and they hated hawks; Billy had seen weasels and coons and some wolves, too, and any of them would have liked a meal of hawk if they could have gotten one. But the crows lacked sufficient courage to attack the hawk nest directly now, with the babies so big, although they often swung close and made a racket and bluffed. The other enemies stayed on the ground and couldn't get close to the nest.

But Billy could. He had thought a lot about it. It would not be hard to climb up there when the parents were gone. He could grab the baby hawk and get out of there, and then—

And then *what?*

This was the problem, and it paralyzed him. He didn't dare take a hawk home. And there was nowhere else. He was stuck. So he didn't do anything at all, and each evening when he climbed to the cliff, he tortured himself with visions of his hawk flying free today—and gone forever.

On a Saturday late in May, Billy became aware of the other trouble.

He was in the garden plot behind the lean-to barn, hoeing weeds from around the corn hills. The thin sunlight felt hot, and dust caked his arms and legs. His father, who had been working on the plow in the side yard, had walked to the front to meet someone coming up the road. But Billy had paid no attention to this until he heard the voices, the first one a little louder than it should have been.

"Everybody has to pitch in, Baker."

"No, not that way." His father's voice.

"Unless we're together on this, it's no good."

11

Curious, Billy put down his hoe and went around the barn and behind the chicken house and along the shallow ditch that ran from there toward the road. He hunched down in the tall grass and got a look at the scene in front of his house.

His father stood near the swing tree, facing three men who had come up on horseback. They had not dismounted, as visitors usually did, and this made the confrontation appear unfriendly. And yet the three men were familiar: Paul Carson, a thick-chested, bearded man who operated the town's biggest general store; Calvin White, the gaunt-faced rancher who was supposed to be the area's wealthiest individual; and a massive older man who operated one of the town's blacksmith shops.

They looked grim. So did Billy's father.

Carson's face worked. "The law isn't getting the job done."

Paw replied, "If it isn't, there are legal ways to make improvements."

"That's what we're talking about. A properly representative vigilance committee."

"That's mob rule, Mister Carson."

"Not with good people running it. Not with all of us together."

"It's still not legal. It's still not right."

Despite the obvious tension, Billy had to smile. The last remark was so characteristic of his father. He was a stern man. Oh, he could have fun, and Billy had seen him laugh —really laugh, startlingly, like a boy. But these moments were few and far between. Dan Baker marched to the drum of a stern God and a law that one did not bend.

Paul Carson and his companions were not smiling. This seemed odd because Billy knew Carson as a friendly, jovial man. He was much different today.

12

"More and more riffraff," Carson said now. "More and more crime. It's time to do something."

Paw nodded. "I had heard there was talk about this. But it's not right. A vigilance committee is no answer to anything. It just means setting up one mob to fight another."

"Nobody said anything about a mob," the blacksmith said.

"It would be a mob," Paw said quietly.

"We're organizing. It won't become a mob."

"Vigilance groups get out of hand."

Carson said, "You've got a reputation for being independent, Dan. A man can admire that. But here we sit, at the far end of the county, with just one deputy, who isn't very smart. The sheriff says he can't afford to send more help. That isn't good enough. We've met. We've talked. We have to act."

"Volunteer as deputies," Paw suggested. "Unpaid."

"That's no good, that's no good!"

"Why?"

"There are things the regular law can't deal with. You know that. While the law is messing with its rules of evidence, these thieves and criminals are stealing us blind. They're carrying off the county. They're providing bad example for our children, making them wild, making them disobey, run crazy, look for trouble. It has to be stopped, and it has to be stopped right now."

Billy thought of Carson's own son, Morrie, almost a man now and yet the wildest boy anywhere in sight with his fights and little group of friends who terrorized younger children and, it was whispered, did other things—much worse things. It seemed odd to hear Carson so excited about law and order when his own son was running crazy.

Paw was saying, "If Sweeney is unsatisfactory as sheriff,

13

there's a lawful way to get him out of there and get a better man in."

"Sweeney is doing darn little for us, and everybody knows it."

"He can be replaced."

"How?"

"You know that answer, Mister Carson. There's an election in late July. If Sweeney is doing a bad job as sheriff, we ought to be looking for a man to run against him. That's the way to deal with a thing like this; you just make matters worse when you start trying to set up your own law."

Carson scowled first at Baker, then at his companions. His jaw worked as he obviously tried to control himself. "We can't wait."

"Then go talk to Sweeney and tell him—"

"We've gone up there and talked to Sweeney until we're blue in the face! He says Plotford is our deputy, and he's all the deputy we're going to get!"

Dan Baker looked up at the three men. The pain was clear on his face. "Then the election in July is the only decent answer."

"You live way out here and you don't go in town much," Carson argued, his face darkening again as the rage worked. "You don't know what it's like. A week ago, a break-in at Purvis's store. On the weekend nights, drunks on the streets, fighting, cussing—womenfolk aren't safe. Two nights ago, Jake Smith was beaten up in the alley right behind the newspaper as he was closing up. A bad element is drifting in, Baker. They're bad people. They're not like us. They're lazy: tramps. They don't work, they're not decent. Word's getting out that they can have a high old time in Springer, and no one will lay a hand on them. Somebody has got to put a stop to it."

14

"How would you do it?" Dan Baker asked, his eyes narrowed.

"Every able-bodied man has to sign an oath to the vigilance committee. Every law-abiding, decent, hard-working man in the valley. That's first. *We've got to be together on this, all of us.* After we all sign, we let the rowdy element know we want them out of the area."

"And what if they don't go?"

Carson hesitated, then set his jaw. "Why, we take action."

"You rough them up?"

Carson's face colored. "Wouldn't be necessary."

"You burn them out?"

"Wouldn't be necessary!"

"How about hanging?"

Carson pointed a finger. "None of that will be necessary, and you know it! Once the bad element sees we're *together* on this, they'll start moving out fast. Think about it as they would. If you're a thief, and you're in our town, and all you've got to worry about is one deputy, you take a chance. Why, you just break into that store. But what if you know *everybody in town* is an enforcer? You know that anyone who sees or hears anything can call out a dozen other men to come running. You'll think twice before you test out the system!"

"People will test it," Paw said. "And members will have to test it, too. That's the way it always works. I've seen this before, Mister Carson, and I *know*."

Carson looked down at Billy's father, and Carson's bearded face showed that he could not understand resistance to his idea. "Join us," he said.

"I'm sorry. No."

The blacksmith said, "You could regret it, you know. A

15

man stands against his neighbors, they might think he was for the other side."

"Oh, I don't think so," Paw said. "You'd have to be really plumb stupid to draw that kind of conclusion, and all my neighbors are smarter than that."

The men looked at each other for a minute. Wind rustled the trees.

Carson said, "I want you to think about it."

"I knew this was coming, Mister Carson. I already have." There was pain in the back of Paw's eyes.

"Think about it more," Carson said.

"Thanks for coming by," Dan Baker said with a thin smile. The pain was deeper in his eyes.

Without more words, Carson flicked reins to turn his horse. The other two men followed his lead. The three riders crossed the yard, ducking under the trees, and turned onto the narrow road. They headed north, not toward Springer but toward the Sled family farm a mile distant.

Dan Baker stood with his old rifle in his arms, watching them.

As Billy scrambled out of the ditch and headed toward his father, the front door of the house opened and his mother came out onto the porch.

Dan Baker turned to look at them and showed a slight smile. "Suddenly I seem to be mighty popular."

"Dan," Ellen Baker frowned, "what does it mean?"

"Maybe nothing. They might just be getting sentiment on the idea—I don't know. I guess we'll see."

"But if everyone else *does* join . . . can we stay out of it?"

"I don't know, Ellen."

Billy said, "If there are bad people around, Paw, wouldn't it be better to make 'em run, like Mister Carson said?"

His father looked at him. *"Would* it?"

16

"I dunno," Billy said, confused by the counterquestion. "But it looks to me like, if there were bad guys around, and all the good people got together, and the bad guys knew all the good people would just really *bust* 'em if they tried anything, then the bad guys wouldn't try anything."

"Okay," his father said. "So if all of us get together and decide to gang up on a bad man, that's a good thing?"

"Right!"

"So what if we all get together and decide to go up the road and burn down the Sled family place?"

Billy was horrified. "No!"

"Why not?"

"Because the Sleds are nice folks!"

"But what if all the rest of us decided we didn't like them anymore? Why couldn't we just go burn them out, just like the other bad man?"

"That wouldn't be *right!*"

"If we *said* it was right, it would be right, wouldn't it? If we can just have a vote on one man, without reference to anything but how we feel, can't we vote on anybody else the same way?"

Billy scratched his ear. He saw he had talked himself into a mouse hole. He also began to see what his father was driving at.

"You can't have it just one way, Billy. It sounds good, people getting together and doing the 'right' thing. But if a mob can take after a bad man, it can take after a good man, too. That's why we have laws. They're so everybody knows what the rules are, and we all go by the same rules. And we elect people to enforce the laws. We're not bigger than the laws. We can't make up our rules as we go along. There are some bad men coming into Springer. I know that. But we can't ignore the law to fight them. Once people start ignoring the laws, nobody is safe: not you, not me, not anybody."

Billy digested it for a moment. It made sense. But part of him protested. It wasn't quite enough. He wanted to be wholly convinced, and he wasn't . . . not yet, anyway.

"But what if Deputy Plotford can't handle stuff?" he asked. "What if ole Sheriff Sweeney won't send in some more help? If there *is* trouble, what do folks do then? Just *set* here?"

Sometimes his father looked quite young, and, under the hardness, oddly vulnerable. It was a sign that he did not have all the answers, and it did not come often, so when it did, it was startling. He had that expression now during a long pause.

"I don't know, boy," he said finally. "I just don't rightly know."

"You don't know?" Billy repeated. "You *acted* like you did!"

"Sometimes you have to make a decision whether you're sure of yourself or not. And I think I'm right about not signing that oath. It's the future I'm uncertain about . . . now."

"Will Mister Carson and those other guys give you a tough time?"

"I don't know that either."

Billy had the feeling that something was slipping away from him. He groped for it. "But you told 'em off—you're really surer than you're letting on, Paw."

. His father smiled glumly. "Sometimes all a man can do is take it one decision at a time—and hope."

It was a shock, this admission of Paw's that he might not *know*. It cast doubt on all his decisions, for if he was unsure *this* time, how many *other* times had he guessed?

18

The thought brought all Billy's uncertainty to the forefront. For the first time, he doubted his father.

He didn't like the feeling this doubt gave, and he tried to wish it away. He had always trusted his father's judgment implicitly—he had been sure that his father could do no wrong. Now Paw had *admitted* he wasn't sure he was doing the right thing all the time, and his action on the vigilance oath made Billy feel a nagging doubt about his father's courage.

Which was ridiculous, doubting Paw's courage. But there the doubt was, and it hurt.

Of course Paw was brave, Billy told himself. And yet he had seen evidence of the problem in town himself, with his own eyes: the fistfight on Main Street that no one dared try to break up with the deputy out of town; the window boarded up after somebody had broken it to get into Steeder's Store; the dark spot on the post office porch that they said had been made by the blood of the old man stabbed and robbed in the night.

If *these* things were not worthy of vigilante action, what was? Was his father right in turning down the chance to help?

Billy was shaken, and his father seemed to sense it.

"Billy?"

"Yes, sir?"

"You *do* understand . . . don't you, boy?"

Billy's throat was dusty. "We better—git this work done, Paw."

He turned and walked toward the garden. He had turned his back on his father, he thought, and he was so confused and upset he couldn't correct it.

They worked side by side at the planting. At first Paw was silent, deeply hurt. But as the back-breaking work went on, he slowly seemed to cheer. Paw was almost always cheerful when he worked hard. Work was what the Good Lord put men on earth for, he said. When he was working hard, he said, he always had the feeling he was getting ahead.

For Billy it was like being closed in a small place. He could not shake his doubts. There was fear there, too. He had seen a certain look in the eyes of the men who had come to call—a look he had seen in nature when a wolf stalked a rabbit with a hurt leg, or the owl swooped upon the mouse. This cruelty in nature was obvious to him, but he hadn't seen it before in men. It seemed, somehow, that men ought to be better than that.

By the time the digging was done, it was almost suppertime. Billy thought of the hawks, and knew it was late in the day to slip off to see them. But he had to do it. Today had been a day when they might fly, and he was anxious to know if they had done so.

Leaving the yard behind the house and barn, he hurried down the slope toward the willow-lined creek, crossed it on the fallen log he always used, and ran out across the meadow to the edge of the woods. He skirted the woods and climbed the steep gully that led to the box canyon. Out of breath from hurrying, he struggled up the steep shale slope of the hill, with the mountain bluish-gray and cloudy above him, and headed for the tree, and the cliff.

It was cool, and starting to get dark. The sun gleamed gold on the face of the mountain high above him. Birds of all descriptions pinwheeled in the evening sky. A rabbit hopped out of tight cover right at his feet, startling him, and zigzagged crazily through the brush and into tree cover. Billy hurried.

The yellow cliff beside the big tree was not quite vertical, but it would have been impossible to climb if it had not been

20

split by a ragged tear in its face. Billy scrambled nimbly up the rocky ditch, climbing the thirty feet that led to the shelf on the cliff face, which was his hiding place.

Here some ancient disturbance had broken a huge chunk out of the rock, and the lip was covered with tumbled boulders, many of them weighing tons. They formed a kind of irregular wall between the cliff face and the dropoff. Billy climbed quickly out among the rocks, leaned head and shoulders between two rounded boulders, and could look down directly into the hawks' nest.

There was only one hawk there. His hawk.

Billy knew immediately what had happened, and his hawk's actions confirmed it. The parents had flown away as usual. The two stronger babies, after days of hopping around on the very edges of the nest, flapping their wings wildly and becoming airborne momentarily, had at last taken the ultimate step—had sailed out beyond the nest and the tree.

His hawk had not taken that last step as yet. His hawk stood on the edge of the nest, flapping wings and crying pitifully, jumping around and shaking the entire nest. The hawk was beside itself with excitement and outrage at being left behind, but it couldn't . . . quite . . . get up the courage to take off. Possibly that first takeoff was always an accident, Billy didn't know.

As he watched, torn between pity and amusement at the dumb thing, he saw his hawk jump so high that it tumbled over backward and rolled all the way back to the deep center of the nest. The hawk gleeped once, got itself back in a sitting position, and settled down, trembling and worn out.

"You poor, dumb ole thing," Billy whispered. "If you'd yelled louder for bugs an' stuff, *you'd* be flyin' and one of them others would be sittin' there."

21

The hawk, as if hearing his soft words, stared up straight at him.

Billy leaned back and studied the sky. Against high clouds, crimson in the setting sun, he spotted a tiny black speck—then another, and then two more. The parents were showing the first two babies how to fly. Or maybe it was just a game. But Billy felt sure that the four specks against the mammoth, distant cloud were the rest of this family, soaring.

Watching them, he felt a chilled pleasure. What would it be like to *fly* like that? To see the ground that far below, and feel the wind from the cloud, and know the gusty, thrusting power of wings as you turned and spun and soared free? To be able to go where you wanted, swifter than anything else in the sky, with all the sky your playground, and to glide through nothingness, testing and knowing every swirl and eddy of air, and see for miles?

Thinking about it and watching the hawks, he felt chill bumps rise.

Below, the remaining hawk creeked in dismay.

"Aw," Billy called down to him, "you'll make it tomorrow, you ole dummy. Don't worry about it."

He was glad to believe that, but the prospect depressed him a little, too. His last chance to have the hawk was just about gone.

Climbing down from the cliffside, he started cross-country, hurrying for home.

His father faced enough possible new trouble, he reasoned, without the added problem of a hawk. It was out of the question to take the hawk home, and that was that. But at least tomorrow, being Sunday, would give him an early start up here tomorrow, and he might get to see the hawk's first flight.

Thinking about this possibility, Billy did not notice the

two horsemen in the grove of trees on the hillside until they rode out very close to him. They were upon him so quickly that he jumped with fright before recognizing them and getting himself under control again.

"Hey, Bobby," the taller of the two young riders grinned to his buddy, "did you see him jump a second ago?"

"I sure did," the smaller, darker-haired youth said. "He scares easy!"

Looking up at Morrie Carson, oldest son of Paul Carson, and Bobby Robertson, whose father was the doctor, Billy felt a pang of resentment. It wasn't the first time they had scared him or some other slightly younger kid. The fact that he had jumped in his surprise, and given them their satisfaction, irked him all the more.

"You guys want something?" he asked.

"We might," Morrie said. His lip curled. "Then again, we might just be out to make rabbits like you jump."

"If you want something, say so. Otherwise you better get outta my way."

"Or what will you do, Billy boy?"

"I don't know. But I've gotta git home, I know that, and—"

"We better let him go right away, then," Morrie Carson told Robertson, "or he'll blubber all the way home."

Billy started past his horse.

Morrie reached down and grabbed him by the shirt collar. The horse moved several nervous strides to the side, hauling Billy off his feet and dragging him.

"Ha!" Morrie yelled.

"Let him go, Morrie!" Robertson pleaded.

Morrie let go, and Billy fell to the ground with shocking impact. He staggered up, tasting dirt in his mouth.

"Don't try to walk off from me again, Billy boy," Morrie

23

warned him. "When I'm through talking to you, I'll tell you so. You got it?"

Billy hesitated. There was a wild, killing light behind Morrie Carson's eyes, which looked a little pale and crazy under the best of circumstances. Morrie wanted an argument now, Billy knew; Morrie wanted an excuse to beat him. It had been that way for years. Morrie had a coterie of friends whom he always led, and they had always terrorized boys just a year or two younger. Now Morrie was grown, practically—was as old and tall and thickset as other boys who had already left Springer to make their own way in the world—and the game was still going on. But now it seemed like being played with by a man, and the possibilities gave Billy a chill that kept him standing there, silent.

"You going to argue?" Morrie asked, his voice rising.

"No," Billy said.

"You just going to stand there like I said?"

"Yes."

"That's because you're yellow, then, Billy boy."

Billy said nothing.

"Yellow," Morrie repeated.

Billy shuddered with the effort to remain quiet.

Robertson said quickly, "Hey, Morrie, he's too scared for it to be any fun, even."

"What do you mean?" Morrie demanded. "The more scared they get, the more fun it is."

"No," Robertson said weakly. "Let's just go—all right?"

Morrie watched Billy, that baleful look in his eyes. A long moment passed. Then Morrie turned his horse abruptly. "Yeah. Let's go. He's too gutless to try *any*thing."

The two young riders went off into the woods again at a full gallop. Billy stood there, the dust settling around him. His humiliation tasted bitter in his throat. The day would come, he thought, when some kind of showdown would be

24

forced upon him with Morrie Carson. There was no way it could be avoided. Today had only been a postponement, so maybe he could grow a little more. Or get a little braver.

He hurried home.

Three

Going to church on Sunday was not something Billy judged in any way; it was just something one did. Set on the edge of the town of Springer, the building was small, painted white, with a small steeple. There were not many windows, which was a blessing in the winter but a bother in the summer, when it became a bake oven inside, and the few windows were open but there was little breeze, and if you glanced out the opened back doors you could see the carriages and horses parked beneath the scanty trees—and the cool-looking mountains and open fields beyond. Going to church was a family thing, and although women outnumbered men, a lot of husbands attended, too. The building was usually crowded, babies wailed, little kids scuffled and sometimes got whapped for their nonsense, the singing was fairly good, and Preacher Wattle gave a long sermon. The sermon was usually the hardest part to get through, but Billy managed by thinking about other things. Sometimes he wondered about the fancy church downtown.

This Sunday, anxious to get away to go see if his hawk had flown, he was more impatient than usual. He noticed that there were more men in the church than normal, but

26

didn't make anything of it. When Preacher Wattle got up on the pulpit and announced that he would talk from Deuteronomy today, Billy settled down between his mother and father, looked serious, and started thinking about other things.

The preacher had been talking ten or fifteen minutes, perhaps, when something alerted Billy to the fact that something was going on. His father, he realized, had stiffened in the pew. His mother was looking across at him—quick, nervous glances—and everybody was really paying strong attention to what the preacher was talking about. Paw's jaw was set in a hard line, and his face looked redder than normal.

Billy perked up and listened.

Preacher Wattle was a short man, rather fat, and when he stood at the pulpit he balanced on tiptoes to lean over. He usually got excited as he spoke, and his voice got shrill. He did not shout, but his hair bushed out and he got a little wild-eyed. He was a little wild-eyed now.

"And so, brothers and sisters," he said shrilly, "the Good Lord sent his chosen people into a new land. He told his people to subdue that land, to obey His laws, to work hard, and to prosper. This was the law of God in those olden times, and it remains the law of our Lord God today. Man earns his way by the sweat of his brow, and if he is righteous, then God will stand beside him."

It sounded puzzlingly like the same old stuff. Billy didn't get it. His father still looked tense, like a man backed into a corner and angry about it. Billy kept listening.

Preacher Wattle balanced on his tiptoes, pushed his belly against the pulpit, and waited a long, impressive moment before resuming. His hair was standing out in all directions, and sweat poured off his face. He raised his hand toward heaven, sort of a half-opened fist.

"And note, brothers and sisters—note *carefully*—how the Good Lord instructed his chosen people in terms of their law and their righteousness. If a man causes a feud in the promised land, he tells them, they are to root out the offender. You are, He told his people, to show no mercy.

"You are to show no pity," the Good Lord said.

"And if there was a false witness, he was to be banished. He was to be banished in a way so that others would hear of it, and know they should not do likewise. Again, God told them: You are to show no pity.

"And then God told them, brothers and sisters, that there might come times when they had to be stern, and take action against evil. He told them that dreadful rule of the just."

Preacher Wattle paused dramatically, and the church was still.

"Life for life," the preacher boomed. "An eye for an eye. A tooth for a tooth. A hand for a hand. A foot for a foot."

Billy saw his mother glance at his father again. But his father did not move a muscle. Jaw set hard, he was staring at the preacher. Billy thought he had begun to get it, and he felt this strange, *vacant* sensation in the pit of his stomach.

"The Good Lord told his people to show no pity in war against injustice," Preacher Wattle went on. "Put the men to the sword, He told them, and take the women and children as booty.

"A stern—yea, even a cruel code, brothers and sisters. And yet it is the word of God. What does it mean to us today? Is there an application in our lives? Can we square this harsh code with the words of the Saviour from Galilee?"

The preacher paused again, took a large white handkerchief out of the sleeve of his black coat, and mopped at his streaming face. The church remained very quiet—no one

28

even coughed—and Billy understood. He was astonished.

"No man," Preacher Wattle resumed darkly, "has the right to take another's life or property. No man or group of men has the right to spoil another's life, or to place him in the proximity of sin. And yet the message of the word of God today, I believe, is that there are occasions when just men must rise up—rise *up,* I say!—to stand against sin and corruption. Against evil, the Good Lord tells us clearly, we must, on occasion, be willing to take a position—the high ground, if you will—and fight.

"I speak of this matter, and have chosen this text, brothers and sisters, because our own fair community may soon face the kind of decision often forced upon those ancient people, those children of a stern God whom we know today through the lesson. To be clear: We have in our own community a growing lawless element. There has been talk of taking action against this element. Some speak of political action. Others counsel more direct action. There is talk of a vigilance committee."

The preacher took a deep breath and looked slowly around the crowd, finally pausing for what seemed an awfully long time on the pew Billy was sitting in. Then the preacher's eyes moved on, and he resumed in solemn tones.

"It is not the place of a church or a man of God to speak of political questions. Render unto Caesar the things that are Caesar's, saith the Lord, and to God the things that are God's.

"As to a vigilance committee, I cannot speak either pro or con. But I can tell you that the word of God itself tells us there are times when action must be taken. Pray over this question, brothers and sisters. That much I do urge upon you. Ask God's help, seek His grace in your minds and hearts. If a peaceful solution to problems can be found, it must be found.

29

"But if, after prayer and deliberation, you decide you must take stern action for the sake of justice and righteousness, then I say to you that God's word does not stand against you. In the face of today's lesson, the word of our Good Lord, no just man can possibly say that direct action against evil is immoral, or sinful, or without blessing by God Himself, and you must pray for justice in your hearts and strength to overcome all travail; and now, brothers and sisters, let us pray."

As Preacher Wattle turned and strode to the altar, Billy was stunned. He felt that the sermon had been directed exclusively at his father—and it seemed totally unfair. You couldn't argue back with a *sermon*.

He risked a glance at his father.

The expression was stubbornly unreadable.

"Well, the handwriting is on the wall."

They were back home, in the house, and Paw stood with his hands on his hips. Mom faced him. Billy stayed as inconspicuous as possible, because the fast, wagon-punishing ride home had told him how upset his father really was.

"On the wall," Paw repeated bitterly.

"Maybe Preacher Wattle wasn't talking about us," Mom said. "Maybe there are a lot of others and we just *feel* that way."

Paw paced up and down. "You go to a church regular. You support it as much as you can. You try to do what the Good Book says. Then they use the church to try to make you do what they want you to do, right or wrong."

Mom frowned and said nothing.

"In front of my own family," Paw said. "In front of my wife and *son*."

"The preacher was giving his opinion, Dan. It's possible he didn't realize he might seem to be singling us out—"

30

"Is it? Is that possible? Did you see that one look he threw at me? Did you see the way people looked at us when we left?"

Mom tried a slight, unconvincing smile. "You did hurry us off fast, and you looked like a thundercloud. Maybe they—"

"No. I thought maybe they'd just leave us alone. But it's clear now they won't. They're going to exert all the pressure they can. That's what makes me sick, knowing this is only the start of it."

"You're upset now." Mom put a tentative hand on Paw's arm. "But—"

"The handwriting is on the wall, I tell you. Paul Carson and that bunch have decided the only way to change things is to mob up, and they're going to use everything they can come up with to force everybody to go along with them. Using the preacher—that was a filthy thing to do. Of course I can't blame Wattle; Carson and his friends are the biggest givers in the collection—"

"Dan!" She was shocked. "He wouldn't *sell* a sermon!"

"I didn't mean that, Ellen. But it's human nature. Carson and his people put Wattle up to it. Now we'll hear from our neighbors, others who'll get pressure put on them, too. They'll build it up. They'll try to force me into joining."

He paused, ran a gnarled hand through his thinning hair, and clicked his teeth together. "If they think I'll knuckle under to that kind of stuff, they're crazy. It's more than just the vigilance committee issue now. I'm a free man, Ellen! I intend to *stay* that way."

"Well . . . maybe it won't be that bad, dear."

Dan Baker turned to Billy. "They'll probably get on you, too, boy. I don't know. Maybe not. But I guess they might."

"What do you mean?" Mom asked.

"Kids will hear their folks talking. Billy will go to school

31

and somebody will say his old man is a coward. So Billy will be supposed to fight."

"If anybody says that," Billy snapped, "I'll—!"

"You don't have to do anything of the kind, boy. You don't have to fight my fight. You don't have to defend me. I don't want to see you coming home with a bloody nose. If you do, then by gosh I'll probably tan you right on top of the whipping you took at school." He pointed a finger. *"Don't* let them suck you into it."

"I won't," Billy said. "But I won't let 'em talk bad about you, neither!"

"Of course, you're off school now until fall. This should have blown over by then. . . ."

"If it hasn't," Billy said, trying to assure himself of his own loyalty, "I'll knock their block off if they say anything about you!"

Billy looked at his father. Their glances locked. Billy held his breath, and then the question came out.

"Paw, *why* won't you sigh the oath? You wouldn't have to ride with 'em—all you'd have to do is say they're okay!"

His father's jaw set like stone. "I saw a mob once, boy. I won't ever support anything like mob action again."

Billy groaned and started to protest that this was no answer at all. But his father's eyes had gone suddenly far away—to that other place and time, and that mob that had somehow changed his life. Billy wondered what it had been, and whether he would ever learn the details. Turning to his mother, he saw that she knew about it, too; her expression betrayed this.

Whatever it had been, clearly, it had been very, very bad.

"If some people want to think I'm a coward," his father said now, stiffly, "let them."

It was a chilling thought that went deep through Billy:

32

Was his father a coward? In nature, a possum avoided death by pretending to be dead already; did cowardly men hide their weakness by *talking* about it, as if it were an illusion?

"Just as long," Paw added, "as you don't think bad of me."

"Is that important?" Billy asked, startled again.

"Of course it is. What do you think a man works for? He wants for his woman to look up to him, and his sons to admire him and follow after him. You're my first-born, Billy, our only child so far. You're *extra* important."

As he spoke, Billy's father squatted in front of him, making their faces at the same level, and close. He squeezed Billy's arm for emphasis, and waited.

Billy was supposed to reassure him, tell him how brave he was, and how sure Billy felt about that. Billy *knew* this was what the silence was for. He felt strangled inside.

Because he couldn't do it. His Paw needed reassurance, and he couldn't provide it. He wasn't even sure how he felt about Paw any more, not right now, and he couldn't lie.

"I better," he said hoarsely, "see about the pets an' stuff."

His father's face reddened as if he had been slapped, and he stood abruptly. "Yes. Good."

He had been hurt.

Billy knew *he* had done the hurting. He couldn't make it better.

Heading for the barn area, he struggled to get the heavy weight off his shoulders. Messing with animals and pets had always been his escape. He had always been able to forget things that bothered him this way. He hoped it worked this time, too, because he felt so terrible.

Rex, the hound, followed him down from the house. As usual, Rex was wagging all over with friendliness and falling down every ten seconds to scratch at fleas. His antics made Billy grin and feel better. "Rex" meant a king, and Billy had always wondered whether Paw had shown a sense of humor or tremendous potential for disappointment in naming the hound that. Rex he was and Rex he would be, but he was no king, boy. He was a good old dog, but the only kingly thing about him was his unmatched capacity for fleas. Paw said if fleas were cows, they would be millionaires.

Crooning the kind of nonsense to Rex that the dog seemed to enjoy, Billy walked around the barn to the area where he kept his pets.

There had been a pigpen in between the barn and the garden once, with hog wire stretched from barn corners to some posts to a couple of gnarled little elms. The fenced area was about thirty feet square, and the pigs were long gone and the fence covered with weeds and pea vines and other dense brush. Billy kept much of the central area hacked down, however, and in this shaded green enclosure he kept the animals.

There weren't really that many. Mom's cats, of whom five or six were presently snoozing in a sunny patch of bare dirt, required no care. They cocked an eye open and watched with the usual distant interest as Billy went to his mouse cages, hung on the barn wall, and checked up on them. He had caught a couple of mice and put them in a knocked-out crate with wire nailed on the ends, just to watch them and study them some. He had given them nesting material and some corn and things like that, and one of them had promptly had babies. By now, Billy had five crates nailed together in a line, with openings cut through the wire here and there. The boxes didn't fit together perfectly in terms of lining up, but this just gave the mice more little crooks and corners to dart around. He had made some blocks and passages in the crates, and when he peered in at the mice, they scurried in all directions, hiding and peeping out at him. He suspected that they really recognized and liked him. After all, he was their source of food, and if there was anything mice were *not* dumb about, it was food. But they sure liked to run when he appeared.

He had fourteen or fifteen mice now.

Using a dipper from the bucket he kept by the barn, he made sure the mice had fresh water in their pans, and checked to see if there was still some of the cake left over from yesterday. There was. Satisfied, he fastened the wire top back on the box arrangement to make sure the cats wouldn't sneak in and have a feast. Then he went across the enclosure to the boxes on the far side, where the rabbits were.

Everybody had said you couldn't box up a wild rabbit, but he had found four of them, babies, out in the field near the creek. He had brought them back and put them in a quilt-lined box. One had died, but the other three had made it. Now, in his two-tiered row of cages made from crates, he had ten rabbits, and by the looks of a couple of them, he was going to have a lot more pretty darned shortly.

Pulling off some weed tops that he had learned the rabbits liked, he stuck them through the wire openings. "Here you go, Big Boy. How's that for supper, huh? Hello, Queenie. How are you doing? Boy, are you ever fat. Don't get rough, Archibald. Just because you're bigger than he is, you don't have to shove him around that way!"

The rabbits took only a few minutes, and then he went to the corner of the enclosure where he kept Alexander the Great.

Alexander the Great had always been a problem. You couldn't keep a raccoon, everybody had said. A coon would dig out or claw out or attack you or go crazy and die, they said. But Alexander the Great had been hurt when Billy found him, and had never been much problem, really.

There was this one problem. Like now. Alexander the Great had dug out again.

His caged area was so dug up it looked like a plowed field, as usual, and his bowl was overturned, food thrown outside, etc. There was one freshly dug hole, and it led to a kind of tunnel that led under the wire and outside, to freedom.

Billy sighed, refilled Alexander the Great's water dish, put in some fresh food, and replaced the lid on the cage.

"Alexander the Great?" Billy called softly.

In the weeds between the pen and the garden there was a sudden rustling, but Alexander the Great did not appear.

"All right, you big ole dummy," Billy called. "I'll give you about one minute, boy, and then I'm going to give your supper to Rex."

The weed patch rustled more fiercely, then there was a flash of gray, and then Alexander the Great shoved in under the wire and through the tunnel and popped his head back up inside the cage. He looked bright-eyed at Billy.

"That's better," Billy said.

Alexander the Great squeezed himself fully up into the cage. He hadn't gone farther than the first fence post for six months, and he was so fat it was ridiculous. He had multiple chins, and if his belly had been a half inch bigger, he would have had to wriggle along like a snake because his legs wouldn't have been long enough. He was one sorry-looking coon, but he was friendly. Looking at the ham bone and old cereal stuff Billy had brought him now, he positively grinned.

"Go ahead, fatso," Billy told him.

Alexander the Great started snarfing in the food. Rex, keeping a polite distance, began yelping and barking and

36

running around as he always did when he saw Alexander the Great getting some food. The mice scurried around in their cages and the rabbits looked up, their noses going a mile a minute, and hopped into the back of their boxes where they did their private things. A couple of the cats even got so excited that they seemed to come out of a coma for an instant, twitch, and seek new positions for a renewed snooze.

"Go on back to the house, you dummy," Billy told Rex. Rex obeyed, loping off.

Billy looked around. Everything was in order here. It was time to go to the mountain.

Heading across the fields, he took another look at the clouds and saw they were definitely nearer. If the storm approached with the usual way of mountain rains, however, he had time yet to visit the hawks' nest and satisfy his curiosity. He kept moving at a steady pace.

He hoped the smallest hawk had flown. That would sort of put an end to it—get his mind off the idea of having a hawk of his own. It was important to get that kind of stuff off his mind. He knew he had to be available if Paw needed him, and he knew he couldn't cause any trouble, even of the smallest kind, at the present time.

It was hard to believe that anything serious might happen as a result of Paw's refusal to join a vigilance committee, but then you could never be sure about folks. They were not as predictable as animals; they might do anything. His father might be in real trouble for all he could guess, and it worried him.

Reaching the hillier terrain, he began thinking more about his hawk and less about other things. He hoped he was early enough to see his hawk's first flight. He had learned enough from nature to know that there was always a runt of the litter. He knew it was silly to feel sympathy for it, but he always did. He didn't know if he *really* wanted to see the hawk fly or not, because when the hawk flew, it became its own creature, free. And yet Billy was telling himself that this had to happen, it was normal, he was dumb to think of might-have-beens.

Going up through the ravine, he saw no hawks, although there were plenty of other birds about. It was warm and sticky and pine-fragrant near the woods. As he approached the cliff near the nesting tree, he caught a flash of red-tan in the deep brush to his left and recognized a young red fox hurrying off for parts unknown. There were not as many foxes around as there once had been. Some of the Indians, it was said, had venerated the fox. But the settlers hated foxes, said they killed too many chickens, and shot them on sight. Now with the foxes declining, there were more wolves here in the high country, and this struck Billy as very strange. Men would never eliminate wolves, he thought, because wolves were too smart. And in the long run they probably killed more things, too. Men would have killed off all the wolves, too, if they could, but wolves were tougher and smarter—and meaner—than foxes. So the fox-killing was just making room for a tougher enemy. It seemed like funny business, but then Billy never had understood all the things grownups did.

Shinnying up the crack in the face of the cliff, he reached his hiding place for observing the hawk nest. Crawling out in the jumble of rocks, he peered down at the nest. It was empty.

He looked carefully, and it was empty, all right, and although he had been prepared for this, he still felt his insides lurch. He had missed the first flight. He would have liked to be there, holding his breath. But he had missed it, and his loss was now definite and final.

Setting his teeth, he looked up at the cloud-gathering

38

sky to see if he could catch sight of anything. There were some birds far away to the north, against the backdrop of the mountains, but they didn't soar like hawks. Nearer at hand he could make out crows.

As he was scanning the sky, he heard some faint commotion below his perch somewhere. It sounded like rocks scrambling. He looked down the sheer drop to the ground below. He could see through the branches of the hemlock to scattered brush and smaller trees below. Here and there the sun got through yellow-bright on rock chips and shale that had come from the face of the cliff itself, and to the right the land sloped sharply down into a deeply shaded gully, which he knew contained a tiny stream and isolated deep pools of water.

He heard the scrambling, thrashing sounds again. They were not far off, and they puzzled him. He couldn't see a thing.

Then, at the edge of his vision, he saw a slow movement in the brush. Riveting his attention on it, he saw the fox coming back.

The fox had his eye on something that Billy couldn't see—something in the brush and rocks of the gully below the cliff. The fox's eyes were very bright, and he moved with infinite care, each paw placing itself very, very slowly and cautiously.

The fox was stalking.

The sound came from the gully again.

Billy scrambled back off his rocky place and went down the crack in the cliff face as fast as he dared, banging up his elbows and knees and sending down little avalanches ahead of him. He ran around the front of the cliff, going underneath the nesting tree. As he got around a couple of big, fallen boulders, he came in sight of the fox at a distance of about twenty feet.

The fox turned and saw him and went stiff for an instant.

"G'wan, you ole fox!" Billy yelled, and swung his arm.

The fox bolted into the deep cover.

Billy moved cautiously forward, headed for the area where the sounds had come from—the place the fox had been approaching. *Something* was in there, probably some creature hurt in some way, he thought. The thought darted across the back of his mind that it *might* be—but he figured that was ridiculous. He moved forward with care, pausing to get a stout length of old broken limb in his hand, just in case.

Some waist-high brush blocked his view into the gully until he moved around it, stick in hand.

There, on the shale incline halfway between his position and the pebbly stream of water a dozen yards below, sat his hawk.

Sat was not quite right, though. The hawk was more *sprawled* on the gravel slope. It faced the other direction, its head was up, and one wing canted outward and down at a decidedly bad-looking angle. Its feathers and remaining fluff were coated with dust and bits of leaves. It was quiet for the first instant Billy saw it, only trembling with fright and excitement.

Then it made a wild attempt to get airborne, flapping its wings furiously and trying to hop. One of its legs didn't support its weight and it rolled over on its side, tumbling a few feet down the slope and getting dirtier and more excited.

"Aw!" Billy gasped.

Without thinking about it, he knew almost exactly what had happened. The hawk had finally gotten into the air from the nest above. It had swooped and soared a little, making a tremendous commotion with a practically uncon-

40

trolled first flight, as hawks often did. Then it had either run smack-dab into a branch or it had gotten into some kind of a spin. Either way—possibly crows were involved somehow—it had come crashing down to the earth, and had hurt itself in the fall.

Now, having made repeated attempts to fly again, it was badly frightened and almost out of energy. The trembling betrayed this. It was hurt, lost, scared, and without defenses.

Which was why the fox had been after it.

The hawk make another flying attempt and tumbled another few feet down the slope. Little rocks and dirt tumbled, making the scrambling sound that had first caught Billy's attention. One more big attempt and the hawk was going right into the stream.

Billy went down the slope fast on his heels, slid to a halt beside the injured hawk, and put a firm hand down on the bird's back, pressing it in place. The hawk turned its head sharply, and its keen, wild eyes studied Billy. It tensed all over and tried to lunge away, but Billy pressed it down more firmly. The hawk had a surprising amount of strength left, but Billy's position let him maintain his hold easily. The hawk struggled another instant, then subsided. Billy could feel its hot body trembling under his hand.

"You're gonna be okay, you ole dummy," Billy crooned. "Just take it easy and we'll figure out what we have to—"

The hawk fought to get free again, not attacking him but writhing and jerking to get loose. It almost succeeded before he managed to fling his leg over the bird's back, pinioning it more tightly.

Upset now about the hawk really going crazy and hurting itself, Billy pinned it with the weight of his bent leg while he snatched his shirt off over his head. Folding the shirt as flat as he could, he tossed it over the hawk and then

41

folded it around to form a sort of sack. He slid one hand under the hawk to try to pick it up in his arms, but through the shirt he was startled to feel the hawk's talons grasp his wrist and hang on.

A little shaky, Billy raised his arm, bringing the hawk up to the level of his chest beneath the shirt. The talons gripped tightly and he could feel their bite—the left clinging considerably tighter than the damaged right—but the grip was not really painful. The hawk, covered up and confused, clung for dear life and did not struggle.

Billy sat down in the sun-warmed pebbles, holding the hawk. He tried to figure out what to do next. He was very excited.

If he let it go again, it was going to keep on trying to fly until it exhausted itself, fell into the stream, hurt itself fatally, or got in a fix where the fox or something else could get it.

He turned and peered up at the huge old hemlock. It crossed his mind that he might try to climb up and put the hawk back in the nest. It was an impossible climb empty-handed, however, and with a hawk on one arm it was out of the question. Even if he might have made it, he had heard that the scent of a human on a wild thing led its parents to reject or even kill it.

So climbing to the nest was impossible for all kinds of reasons.

Climb the cliff, maybe, and put the hawk on a safe-looking shelf? It was hurt. It would starve. Or something would get it there, too.

The only thing in the world to do, Billy thought, was take the hawk home with him. But he had his orders about *that,* and Paw had enough troubles.

What, then?

The hawk stirred on his arm, slightly clasping and un-

42

clasping those strong talons, redistributing its weight. It was really not such a big bird yet. It was completely helpless. Billy felt such a sudden burst of sheer love for the dumb old thing that he was jolted.

Whatever he did was going to be awfully, awfully wrong. He could try to save the hawk and disobey his father. Or he could leave the hawk and try to *pretend* it wasn't going to die as a result.

"Caught between the devil," he had heard his father mutter once in disgust, *"and the deep blue sea."*

Precisely.

But he had to do something. That was the worst of it. He couldn't just sit here forever like a stump. *Come on, brain, think!*

The more he thought about it, the worse the alternatives looked. He knew wild animals died violently, and often young. He knew it was nature's way to take the weakest. He knew he was a silly fool to get involved.

But it was *his* hawk, and—

Overhead, a sudden slight commotion caught his attention. Looking up, he saw the adult red-tails swoop back to their nest. The two younger hawks turned and swung through the trees, and followed. The family preened and moved around and started to settle down for a rest or food, Billy couldn't tell.

His hawk clung to his wrist. Quiet, out of it, and depending totally upon him.

Billy got awkwardly to his feet, balancing the hawk under the shirt, and trudged up the gravel slope. The sun burned into his bare back. He knew he was going to regret this, but he just had to do it.

Four

By late afternoon, Billy had done everything he could. He knew it was not going to be enough unless he found some kind of help. Under the circumstances, there was only one person he could ask.

"Where are you going?" his father called as he started across the yard for the road. His father was working under the wagon, trying to brace a spring or something, and Billy could see only his legs sticking out.

"I'm just going up the road a while," Billy told the legs.

"To the Sled place?"

"Yes, sir."

Pause. Then: "If they ask you about the vigilance committee or anything like that, boy, remember what I told you."

"Yes, sir."

"No fighting."

"Yes, sir."

Another pause. Then: "Maybe they won't mention it."

"Yes, sir," Billy said.

The hammering resumed under the wagon.

Feeling more guilty than ever, Billy walked up the road.

44

The sun beat down hotly, but rainclouds were much closer now, and he felt sure it would be teeming down by nightfall. That made his errand seem more vital.

It was going to be his first visit anywhere since becoming aware of the Big Problem concerning his father, but the *other* problem drove him. Possibly, he told himself, the Sleds wouldn't mention the vigilance committee. They were good folks, always had been. And Jeremy was his best friend. He had to count on Jeremy . . . had to take the chance.

The Sled farm was even smaller than Billy's, and the house poorer. It was a soddie, dug out partially in the side of a hillock and then built up with great earthen walls cut with a spade from the virgin grass. At a distance it looked like a log house, and indeed Mister Sled was building a log one, but its skeleton stood lonely some fifty paces from the little hill, and work had been abandoned until the crops were in or some money came from somewhere. The soddie, with its earthen walls and roof, looked brown and shaggy and substantial, yet about to fall down, as one walked closer to it. Only the barn and storage shed looked permanent. The yard was littered with toys and junk strewn around by the many Sled children, and a broken plow stood rusting near the badly fenced garden. Several of the smaller children were playing in the dirt near the garden. Billy noticed, as he walked up, that the Sled garden was a little ahead of the one he and his father were getting in: The corn was up here, about two inches high already, and the cabbages were starting to make.

Walking up near the black, open front door of the soddie, Billy took a breath to call and caught the characteristic earthy odor of the interior. He could hear more kids inside.

"Jeremy," he called.

Inside, Mrs. Sled's voice came: "Jeremy, Billy is outside."

Jeremy appeared in the doorway. He was a year older than Billy, and a foot taller. Until a few months ago he had been the same size, and chubby. Now he was over six feet, a scarecrow figure, all bones and angles and extremities sticking out of shirts and pants too small for him, with yellow hair and protruding teeth and bare feet and a lazy, insolent smile. He had always been a basically kind person, though, both when he was four feet, eight, and when he had suddenly become six feet, one.

"Hullo, Billy," he grunted.

"Got a minute?" Billy asked.

"Yuh, I guess so. I ain't doing nothing."

"What would you say we, uh, walk out the back?"

"Yuh, okay."

They walked around the side of the soddie, along the ridge of earth into which it was built, then onto the flat ground by the barn. To the right, in the distance, was Billy's place and the mountains beyond. Straight out behind the Sled place, the prairie just seemed to extend for a million miles into infinity. Jeremy, hands in his pockets, looked dully at the infinity of grass and then kicked at a pebble.

"What you doin', Billy?" he asked.

"I've got a problem," Billy told him quietly. "I need some advice."

"Yuh?"

"Yeah, I'm afraid so. I've got a hawk, and I don't know what to do with it."

"You got you a hawk? Aw! You always was lucky, as well as smart with critters."

"I don't know if this is lucky or not," Billy admitted. "See, my paw said I couldn't keep him at the house. But I can't just leave him in the woods, he's hurt. So—"

"Where is he at now?" Jeremy interrupted.

"Well, I've got him in the woods, in a box, covered up with old rags to keep him quieted down. But I can't leave him that way too long. He's got to have himself some exercise. And if I'm gonna keep him, I got to train him, too . . . some, anyway. And I don't know anything about it."

Jeremy nodded. "You got a problem, sure enough."

"What do you think?" Billy asked.

"What do *I* think?" Jeremy was astonished.

"Is there anybody that knows a lot about hawks? Do you know about any expert hawk person in the valley—so maybe I could take this ole hawk to him, and leave him, so he wouldn't die?"

Jeremy scratched his head for a while. "The only person I ever heard of that was a hawk person," he said finally, "is the crazy man. And then I ain't sure, but I did hear it somewheres."

"The crazy man!" Billy gasped.

"Well, you know, they say he keeps lots of critters."

Billy thought about it a moment. "I can't ask the crazy man!" he said finally. "That would be—*crazy.*"

"He might take the hawk, though."

"He'd probably *eat* it!"

Jeremy did not smile. "Dunno."

Billy thought about it some more. He was shaken.

The town of Springer had always had a crazy man, people said. Once, last year, there had been three at once, including a one-eyed black man who lived in the river bottom and ate wild grapes and nuts. Right now there was only one crazy man, but he was quite enough.

The current crazy man lived in the mountains north and west of Springer. He squatted on the side of one of the

47

mountains, where, it was said, he had a cabin inhabited by dozens of wild animals. He looked fairly wild himself: long hair going to gray, woolly beard that stood out all around, penetrating dark eyes, and a voice that could boom, they said, when it yelled from a distance. The crazy man stayed to himself and never did anything as far as anyone could tell, except that he did go into town about quarterly to get salt and a few such basics. He had cash money.

"If you don't try the crazy man," Jeremy told Billy, "I guess I got no suggestions fer you. He's the only one *I* ever heard of thet might he'p with an ole hawk."

"Have you ever seen this crazy man?" Billy asked.

"Shoot, no!" Jeremy looked startled.

"I haven't either. I don't know if I want to, either."

"You afraid?"

"I might be," Billy admitted heatedly. "Want to make something of it?"

Jeremy looked down at him and grinned. "I might be too," he admitted.

"Maybe you could just take the hawk," Billy began. "I could feed it and all, see, all you'd have to do is sort of pen it and hide it—"

"Nope," Jeremy said quickly. "Ain't *no* way. My daddy said if I brang in any more critters, I'd haf to skin 'em an' eat 'em for supper, he'd make me."

Billy took a deep breath. "I sure *hate* to think about that crazy man."

"Well, he probably ain't very crazy, you know. He's probably jus' a ole hermit."

"*Sure.*"

"An' I sure can't think of anything *else* you might try."

Billy nodded and started to turn away, worried.

48

"Hey," Jeremy grunted. "What'd you think of that sermon this mornin'?"

"Not a whole lot," Billy said, rudely reminded.

"Yur daddy won't sign the vigilance pledge, huh?"

"Nope."

"Well, my daddy first said he'd sign it, but then he heard how your daddy wasn't, so now mine ain't signing neither."

"Is that right?" Billy said, delighted.

"Yep. I hear tell Mister Dodge won't sign, neither, an' some folks on the far side of town said no, too. I guess that's why the preacher got hisself all lathered up this mornin'. They's enough people sayin' no right now, my daddy says, that they can't be sure of havin' a good committee. So they're gonna try mighty hard to git folks in, my daddy says. He said he was agoin' go down an' see yur daddy this evenin'."

"My paw will be glad to see him, Jeremy. He's been thinking he was all alone on this deal."

"Nope, I don't think so. I think as long as yur daddy holds fast, it gonna give some other folks the idea to hold fast, too."

Billy felt better and grinned. "Good."

"So what about the hawk?" Jeremy demanded, bringing him back to reality.

"I dunno," Billy said.

"The crazy man's yur onliest hope," Jeremy pronounced solemnly.

"You might be right."

"You gonna take thet hawk up there to him, then?"

"I've got to *think* about it first."

Thunder rumbled across the big sky. Jeremy squinted at the clouds and held out his hand, catching a raindrop.

"Don't think about it too long," he said cheerfully. "Yur

ole hawk might git hisself drownded before you've made up yur mind."

The rain began steadily about six o'clock, and then pelted down in earnest starting well after dark, when Billy was already up in the sleeping loft. He lay in the dark and listened to the heavy drops hammer against the roof only a foot over his head, and he imagined the hawk in the box he had rigged out in the woods as near the house as he had dared place it.

The box was nailed to the tree, and fitted into a crotch so it could not fall. The lid was tight, nailed in. Billy had left only a few airholes, nothing large enough for the hawk to see out of—or be attacked through. And he had had the foresight to put some roofing paper over the box; it would not get too wet inside.

But poor hawk! The tree was going to sway in this wind, which now whistled over the roof and chimney, and rattled things distantly in the barn. Some rain was going to come in, and the hawk was going to hear the howl of the wind, too. He was going to be scared, Billy figured.

After a long time of heavy wind along with the rain, the wind began to subside and the rain intensified, pounding with a dull steadiness that was a continuous roar. Then, again later, Billy roused from worried sleep to hear the rain light on the roof, showing that the storm was continuing to pass. Knowing that the worst was over for his hawk by now, he dropped off to deeper rest.

In the morning, little rivers and rivulets ran through glistening mud in all directions in the front yard and garden. A limb was off the front tree, and there were small elm leaves everywhere. The garden looked beaten, the small plants bent over and dragging in puddles, but they would come back. Everything looked beaten now, but the rain

50

would work magic in the long run. It had been needed. The earth glistened, the bare mud gleamed. The wet odor was fresh and bracing.

Paw stood at the window, hands on his hips. "No farming today, boy."

"Yes, sir," Billy said, forcing a smile.

"Inside work today, and maybe later some relaxation." Paw turned and looked at Billy, and Billy instantly looked away, embarrassed and uneasy.

Paw was thinking about checkers this afternoon, he thought. They did that, sometimes, on bad days: worked in the house and the barn in the morning, then hunkered over the board near the fire in the afternoon. It was always good, by the fire, with the smell of Paw's pipe in the room.

It wouldn't work today, though, and in the instant their eyes met and slid off, they both knew it. Their relationship was too strained. It all went to the vigilance committee questions, Billy thought. *And it's all my fault for not having faith!* he thought.

His father sighed. "Something you'd rather do today than help me?"

"I've got . . . some stuff to do with the pets an' all," Billy lied.

"All right. Do what your mother wants done. Then go."

His mother did not have a long list of chores for him, and despite his depression, he got them done in record time. Before eleven o'clock he was finished with all of it and headed out across the icy-wet meadow, his boots already clogged with heavy mud.

He needed all the time he could get, he thought, if he was to find the crazy man and still have a chance of getting back before dark.

His first stop was the spot in the woods where he had hidden the hawk in its box yesterday afternoon. He approached the location carefully, and with worry, because any number of things could have gone wrong: The storm might have knocked the box out of the tree despite his best nailing; the hawk could have been badly hurt to start with, and simply died; something *might* have gotten into the box and eaten him; the hawk could even have escaped, and managed to get far enough away on the ground not to be findable. Any number of other things could have gone wrong, too. So Billy approached not only cautiously, but holding his breath with a kind of dread, at least until he spotted the box firmly in its place, the lid seemingly intact.

Moving quietly up to the box itself, he assured himself that he needn't have worried. His shirt still formed a good curtain inside the box. He raised a little corner of the shirt on the box, letting in some light. The hawk flustered around inside, making a big racket. Billy quickly restored darkness, satisfied about the hawk's strength this morning.

The whole idea of approaching the crazy man was bad enough, of course, but the idea of carrying the hawk box halfway around the world, it seemed like, was even worse. There just wasn't any help for it. Billy knew he had to locate the crazy man himself, and he had to take the hawk along by himself. He didn't have any options, since Jeremy was the only person he could have even asked to come along, and Jeremy had been pretty definite about avoiding the crazy man.

Working gently to avoid frightening the bird, Billy got the box loose from its moorings in the crotch of the tree, then safely on the ground. He rested a couple of minutes, but then, knowing he didn't have any time to waste like this, he picked up the box again. The only way he could carry it securely was against his chest, which was awkward, and required both arms. No help for that, either.

Heading north and east, Billy took the shortcuts he knew

well in the local terrain. After about an hour he was just about out of familiar territory, but by this time he had already crossed the river and was beyond town. Rain clouds hung against the sides of the mountains like gray-blue blankets, but no rain yet fell.

Although Billy did not know exactly where the crazy man's place was, he had a good general idea. He moved up the foothill slopes, working through conifer forests, and out the far side onto sloping grassland studded with big boulders. As he trudged upward, holding the hawk box awkwardly against his chest, he could tell he was making progress because his breathing began to get harder—the altitude. He was tired, too, but it would be worth it if he could get the hawk cared for.

If the crazy man was unable or unwilling to help, Billy had no idea what he might do. Maybe he would take the hawk right up to his home, tell Paw what had happened, and hope for mercy. Maybe he would come up with some other idea; no telling. He was pretty amazed that he was actually doing *this*—going to see the crazy man, and it sort of showed the things you could think of, and do, if you had to.

After an hour or so of climbing, with the rain a dense mist in the air and so cold it made Billy's lungs throb with every breath, the crazy man's house came into view. No one else had anything this high on the mountain, so Billy knew what it was the moment he spotted it.

He had climbed into more woods, and was making his way across a shelf when he saw the crazy man's place ahead. It was situated against a dirt cliff, and appeared to be either a dugout or an old cave dwelling with a new door arrangement, the ax-hewn logs forming the front wall yellow in the gray light. Two small log outbuildings and a pen stood nearby, equally protected by the slightly overhanging

53

cliff, which was enormous. Some junk—a few tin cans, some buckets, rolled wire, and broken boxes—lay around here and there, but in general it was a remarkably neat camp for a man who was supposed to be crazy.

Not seeing the crazy man anywhere in view, Billy made his way down off his vantage point, through the brush and timber, and into the clearing around the camp. He was glad to be here since his arms were about dead from hauling the box, but his insides quaked a little with nervousness, too. He *supposed* the crazy man was friendly. Until now it hadn't occurred to him to ask, though.

A little late, everything considered.

Billy walked across the clearing, passing the pen situated between the two main sheds. A fawn stood quietly in the pen. One of her legs was splinted and bandaged neatly with rags. What was amazing was that she looked right at Billy and didn't appear very nervous at all. On the side of the larger shed there was a shelf, and a big brown owl stared from this perch sleepily. A couple of squirrels sat on the roof, arguing over a nut. Billy had the strange feeling that they—and the bright bird in the nearest tree—belonged here as much as the obviously penned fawn. But there was still no sign of the crazy man.

"Hello?" Billy called, not too loud, so as not to spook any critters.

No reply. The squirrels sat quiet, having settled their fuss about the nut. In the distance came some thunder.

Sighing with relief, Billy put the hawk box on the steps that led up to the boarded entry of the dugout or cave house. It felt mighty good to let his arms slide to his sides.

"Anybody home?" he called louder, facing the front door.

Something rustled behind him—possibly cloth against a rock—and a feathery shadow went over his head. Startled, he began to turn. The shadow became a light but strong

54

rope that sang over his shoulders and around his waist, pinning his arms to his sides as the noose was jerked closed.

"That's enough!" a male voice boomed behind him. "Just don't try to get away, there, young feller! Just stand still, now, I mean business!"

Tingling with fright, Billy didn't fight the rope, but he did turn toward the voice.

Coming into view from behind the larger shed, the crazy man kept the rope in his hands taut as he sort of wound it up from where he had tossed it over Billy's shoulders from hiding. The crazy man looked very excited and upset, his long hair standing out in all directions, his beard bristling, sweat glistening on his high forehead.

He was a fairly large man, the crazy man was, with a slight beer belly protruding through the baggy covering of his gray flannel shirt. He wore black pants, very old, and clodhopper-type shoes, the kind that laced up the side, and a pearl-colored vest with yellow lining. His shaggy hair and beard made his head look even larger than it was, and it was large to begin with—heavy, lionlike. If he looked a little like a lion, then it was a pretty old lion, because Billy could tell the crazy man was sixty if he was a day.

"Just don't think you'll get away, feller," the crazy man said, hopping around Billy and keeping the rope taut. "You'd better just stand still!"

"I am!" Billy protested. "I'm just standin', see?"

"What did you think you'd do, eh? Come up here an' bother the crazy man, eh? Steal his pets? Throw rocks through his window, eh?"

"Did somebody do that stuff?" Billy asked, amazed. He swiftly imagined how some of the older boys might have figured it was a good joke to come up here and heckle a man who was supposed to be crazy anyhow—

"Fooled you this time," the crazy man chuckled, still

55

dancing around to keep the rope taut. "Yes, indeed! Yes, indeed! Fooled you! Caught you! Now what have you got to say for yourself?"

"I didn't come to cause trouble," Billy growled. "I came to see if I could get some help from you."

"Help?" the crazy man repeated, cocking his head at a wild angle and rolling his eyes. "How's that you say? Help? What do you mean, feller, by help? What kind of prank did you plan to play on the old crazy man, eh?"

"I brought that there box," Billy said. He was getting over his initial fright and was getting irritated now. Somehow he just didn't think the crazy man was a threat, and he wanted to get the sparring over. "See this box? *That's* why I came."

"What's in it?" the crazy man snapped, turning up his nose. "Skunk?"

"No."

"What, then? Something to throw in my house?"

"No! It's a young hawk. A red-tail."

"In that box?" The crazy man frowned, his eyes alert.

"It fell," Billy said. "Hurt itself."

"And you come to me? Why?"

"My friend said he heard you was good with critters. My father says I can't have any more wild things at our house. I didn't want to just let this hawk die—"

"What's your name?" the crazy man asked.

"Baker, sir. Billy Baker."

"And you have you a hawk in this here box?" Suspiciously, trying to find an angle, as if he had trusted once too often already.

"Yes, sir."

The crazy man, frowning, came to the porch steps, put his weight on one knee, and very gently raised a corner of the box to peer inside. He looked sharply up at Billy, then

56

bent to peer into the box again. He reclosed the lid and stared into space, evidently flabbergasted. "You come to *me.*"

Billy said nothing.

The crazy man quickly—gently—pulled the rope from around Billy's arms and lifted it over his head, freeing him. "Sorry about this rope. You okay? You hurt?"

"I'm fine. You scared me for a second."

"Meant to," the crazy man grunted with satisfaction. "Oh, not *you,* of course; the ones that've been comin' up here, tossing rocks at my fawn, throwing garbage around. Guess they think it's funny, messing everything up."

"I just brought this here hawk," Billy assured him.

"Right, right. I see that now." The crazy man's face and eyes were gentle, pleased, and thoughtful. "My name is McGraw, sonny. You can call me Mac or you can call me McGraw. I'll take it very personal if you call me the crazy man, though, leastwise to my face."

"Pleased to meet you, Mister McGraw."

"Pleased to meet you, too, sonny."

"About the hawk, sir—"

"Yes, yes, yes. Nice-looking young hawk. You say he's hurt? You want to tell me about it?"

"You can help, then?" Billy asked, half dreading the reply.

"Of course I can!" McGraw said.

"You know stuff about hawks?"

"I know," McGraw smiled, *"everything* about hawks."

Not quite willing yet to believe his good luck, Billy told McGraw everything he knew about the hawk. He left out nothing, and by the time he was through talking he was a little hoarse from all the words under strain of excitement.

57

McGraw had watched him keenly through the recitation, paying very close attention both to him and his story.

"You observed everything you've told me?" McGraw asked finally. "Or is some of it more or less made up?"

"No, sir," Billy snapped. "Except for my theory about how he got hurt, I saw all of it."

"You've done you a lot of observing, sonny."

"I guess so, sir."

"You must like wild things."

"Yes sir, I sure do!"

"Most boys your age figure a wild thing is just a moving target for a gun."

"I'd never shoot something like a hawk!"

McGraw smiled faintly, as if disbelieving, then shook his head as if to assure himself of reality. "Tell me this, sonny: What do you want to do? Get this hawk healed up and then let him go?"

"That's probably what it will come to," Billy admitted. "I mean, that would be plenty. If you could just help me get him—"

"Wait a minute, wait a minute, now. You act like there's *more* you'd like to do with this hawk. You want to tell me about that?"

"Well," Billy admitted, "I've heard about training hawks."

"Training them?" McGraw's keen eyes sparkled.

"To fly free—to come back when you call," Billy said. "To hunt for you!"

"Falcon can learn some of that," McGraw said, his eyes alive with amusement and speculation. "It's not as easy to train this kind of hawk to act that way."

"I'd sure like to try, though," Billy breathed. Then, catching himself: "I mean I know I can't do it with *this* hawk.

My paw made that clear. But boy, *some* day—think of it! To really train one—"

"Not an easy job," McGraw snorted gently.

"I guess not," Billy admitted. "I dunno how you do it —do you?"

"Aaagh, I've trained a few hawks in my time, if it comes to that."

"You *have?*" Billy cried. "Then you could—I mean, *could* you—"

McGraw twisted his face as if he were in pain. "Now, *listen,* boy! We don't even know if your stupid hawk is going to live. I haven't even examined him yet!"

"Do you want to examine him now?" Billy asked excitedly.

McGraw threw up his hands. "Bring the box into the small shed."

The shed had contained birds of some kind before. It was hot and dim and closed off to most outside light, and the odor was of bird dung and feathers. McGraw had Billy place the box in the center of the floor, and while Billy was doing this, McGraw brought some kind of small object out of a far corner. Billy saw that it was a leather-covered perch, formed by covering a T-shaped branch and handle, the butt of which fitted neatly into a hole bored in the floor planks. Some thin leather straps and a larger leather pouch of some kind were attached to the perch.

"All rightee," McGraw said softly, turning from the perch after he had it set up. "You just stand back a couple of steps, there, sonny. Against the wall. That's it. I'm going to take your little hawk out, now, and get him organized and inspected. It's no job for a boy. It can be dangerous—even," he added quickly with a meaningful look, "for a boy as expert as you are."

Billy was pleased by the compliment and not about to

59

interfere in McGraw's ways of doing things, so he backed off against the wall and watched.

McGraw carefully and slowly lifted the lid of the crate, sliding his hand inside as he did so. Although the light in the shed was dim, it probably seemed bright to the hawk after the box. The hawk started to panic. McGraw got his hand on the hawk's back and sort of held it down while he finished taking the lid off and removing Billy's shirt curtain.

"Bird's a little thin," he remarked calmly, reaching back with his free hand to get something off the perch.

"He was the runt—" Billy began.

"*Shhhh*, now."

Billy watched. McGraw expertly maneuvered a small leather pouch with his free hand, slipping the pouch over the hawk's head. His fingers slipped it into place on the first try, and somehow or other he managed to tie the two small strings to keep it in place, doing it one-handed quicker than Billy understood what he was trying to accomplish. The hawk struggled against the hood for an instant, but then, fully blinded again, settled down.

McGraw gently picked the hawk up and sat it on the perch. The hawk hung on and stood erect.

With a series of quick, gentle movements, McGraw examined the hawk. Then he flipped two light, thin leather loops around the perch and got them fastened to the hawk's legs with sure movements. Then he stood stiffly, rubbing his back and looking down at the hawk with consideration and thought.

"Like I said," he muttered, "he's sorta thin. Wing is hurt some, but not bad. Leg, too, on the same side. But he holds the perch all right, and he didn't flinch too much when I got the *jesses* on him. I'd say there's nothing major wrong with that bird at all, young feller."

Billy stared at the hawk on its perch, hooded and prop-

60

erly fastened down, just like it had been hooded and fastened that way all its life, and he was as amazed as he was thankful. "You just *put* him there—and there he stays?"

McGraw chuckled. "He's tired and confused and some hurt right now. He might fight the *jesses* later. He might as well learn one time as another."

Billy stared at the hawk again, and McGraw nudged him to leave the shed. "C'mon. Let's let this hawk rest."

Outside, Billy squinted in the blinding sun. "You'll help the hawk get better, then?"

"Well, I'll try. I got nothing else in the building right now anyhow. A few weeks ago you'd of been out of luck. I had these snow owls. But they're fine, all flew off."

"You think this hawk will get okay, though," Billy insisted.

"I wouldn't be at all surprised."

"Then you'll . . . you might let me learn how to train him?"

"Now, *that's* a different deal," McGraw said firmly. "Training a bird of prey is dangerous. It takes technique. Sometimes there are birds that won't train. Sometimes you train one perfect, get it right to the end of its training, and it takes off and heads for the tall timber—and that's it, you never see it again."

"But I could sure work hard," Billy said eagerly, "if I had help."

"Sometimes the bird goes bad," McGraw went on somberly. "It works well for a while, then goes sour overnight, sulks, flies off."

"I can get up here just about every other day, some time," Billy said. "See, I've got to work with my paw, and sometimes my mom has jobs for me to do, too, and I've got the coon and rabbits and mice and cats and Rex to feed and water, but I could get away *pretty* often, I could run most of the way—"

"And what will your parents think, you coming to visit the crazy man?"

"I didn't think I'd tell them," Billy blurted.

McGraw's fine white teeth showed. "Just lie, huh?"

"No, sir! Just—well—just *not tell*."

McGraw shook his head slowly, walked around his campsite, and kicked a log. "Looks to me like a bad deal all around. The bird goes bad, you're disappointed. Your folks find out you're coming up here, you get tanned, and I get burned out or something equally silly."

"There won't be any trouble," Billy said. "I *promise*."

McGraw soberly tapped him on the chest with his index finger to emphasize the point. "Your parents object, you got to quit coming."

"Yes, sir!"

"The hawk goes bad, we let him go."

"Yes, sir!"

"You do what I tell you, see, because I know hawks."

"Yes, sir!"

"You recognize the hawk will probably disappoint you—I don't want any hysterics around here if it just flies off."

"Yes, sir! Right!"

McGraw glowered at him. "You like cookies?"

Startled, Billy didn't understand. "Sir?"

"I said—oh, tarnation—come on in the house!" McGraw turned and strode up the porch of the cave-dugout, jerked it open, and went in. He had to bend slightly to duck the ceiling.

Following him, Billy went into a large, single room that indeed had been an ancient cave dwelling of some kind. The rock walls and floor sloped gently toward the back,

62

where they finally met somewhere in the darkness beyond the light that funneled down from a tall shaft in the rock overhead. The hole looked fifty feet over Billy's head, and it might have been a natural chimney or it could have been cut by ancient users; at any rate, it provided both light and ventilation for the big room.

McGraw's furniture was very simple, all of it made right here on the hillside: a lamp from an old tin can; a stove for cooking, also made from cans; some box tables and box chairs; and a bed rigged from ropes and chunks of ax-squared logs. What struck Billy hardest was how very, very neat and clean the dwelling was, cleaner than any house he had ever been in, even his own. It was like the home of an animal, he thought, but the animal was very smart and very clean.

McGraw gruffly ordered him to sit at a crate table, using one of the lower boxes for a chair. He brought him some cookies on a chipped plate and some water out of a storage can that wasn't really cold, but wasn't warm, either.

Billy tasted one of the cookies to be polite, and learned it was just about the best cookie he had ever stuck between his teeth. "Hey! These are *great!*"

"Of course they are," McGraw grunted. "I made 'em, didn't I?"

For a crazy man, Billy thought, he was awfully smart.

Five

It was an uneasy feeling, having a secret.

Billy's impulse was to tell his parents about the old man, and taking the hawk to him. But he kept quiet about it. At first he sensed that his father's reaction would be bitter— a denunciation for disobeying, followed by an ultimatum about getting the hawk back and turning it free . . . and then the hiding in the shed. But fear quickly passed into something else, a secret knowledge that, in this one thing, *he might know better than his father.* Billy had never had this feeling before, and it was disconcerting; he did not know if it was to be trusted. But he obeyed the feeling and said nothing.

On Tuesday, the family went into town for the week's shopping.

It was always a major event, the highlight of the week, even though the shopping seldom amounted to many items. It was an occasion when his father mingled with other men, and could be heard talking about crops, the weather, prices, the cattle market, and other arcane matters. Billy's mother could always be counted upon to make her shopping last much longer than seemed sensible, dawdling

64

endlessly over a bolt of cloth or a card of buttons. Billy usually got stuck with his mother, but sometimes he got to stand outside with his father and listen to the talk.

Springer was a small town, but fairly self-contained. It was in one of the valleys, beside a creek, and it had trees even along wide, dusty Main Street. You came into the town rather suddenly, up the lumpy dirt road over the timbered creek bridge, through a grove of trees, and to a slight rise where rooftops could be seen in the trees ahead, then down past a few log or clapboard houses strung along the roadway, past a weed field in which a chimney stood, fire-blackened, over rubble, and then around a bend and onto Main Street itself.

Main Street—the wide part—was two blocks long, with one street intersecting in the middle, where one church put up its steeple against the mountain sky. The first part of the block was barns and storage buildings, and some empty lots. The street got busier as one approached the church corner. On one side were Carson's Store, flanked by the gunsmith's shop and Tella's Dress Shoppe on the left and Doc's Confectionery and Springer Feed and Seed on the right. The far side of the street was also busy, and included the post office, the barber shop, three saloons, and the enormous clutter of Bainbridge's Hauling Company. The commercial buildings sort of petered out near the fancy church, as if out of respect, and the area immediately around it was broad and grassy. But on beyond the church were more one-story buildings, including, well up at the end of the next block, the jailhouse. Billy had never been to the jailhouse.

He had never been to the fancy church—his mother's description—either. Their church was more modest, and on the outskirts, along the side road. That was the road that led to the bigger, grander houses belonging to some of the

65

merchants and to the banker. The bank was on the side street not far from the fancy church.

All of this suggested to Billy, from time to time, and vaguely, that Springer was not the simple community he had once imagined. He knew that there were *layers* of people in the town: the drunks and the drifters and others who got arrested a lot on the bottom, and then probably the cowboys and others who sometimes didn't stay long but seemed to spend a lot of money, and then the sheepmen, and then the start of the *real* people: the farmers like his family, and then the merchants like Mister Carson, and then folks like the banker, and then the preacher and school-teacher and people like that, way up there on the top, practically out of sight. The fact that these layers existed did not bother Billy much, though. He knew his layer was the best.

The street was fairly active on the sunny Tuesday they drove in this time. Several horses, saddled, were tied along the rails in front of the saloons. Two large wagons and five smaller ones were scattered along the side of the street near Carson's and the feed store. There were some farmers standing in the roadway talking, and kids playing in the dirt, and several women bustling around on the board sidewalk or going into stores.

As usual, Billy was riding in the back of the wagon, his parents on the slab seat in front, and he hunkered to the side to greet people as his father pulled the wagon up between two others. The smells of dust and manure were heavy in the thin air. Billy glanced around, seeing a number of familiar families, but none of the kids his own age he was seeking. Some of the younger kids waved to him. He waved back.

Then, as the wagon was halted, and the horses settled in, clomping and shifting in their harness, Billy realized that everything was not quite normal.

66

The first thing he noticed was the *quiet*.

Several groups of people had been talking when they pulled up. But for just an instant, as the team settled, the conversations slacked, and he saw a number of faces turn to stare for an instant, then turn away again.

His father set the hand brake and swung down off the seat, walking around to help Mom down. Nobody said anything, although a number of the private conversations got started again, all at once. Billy looked hard at his father and saw that his face, under the shade of his hat, was set in a way that said he was all squinched up inside, not quite angry, but sort of on the defensive.

Paw helped Mom down. Mom *seemed* not to notice anything. She caught one of the nearby ladies' eye. "Hello there, Mrs. Madison!"

Mrs. Madison, an older lady wearing a sunbonnet, hesitated just an instant, then smiled. "Hello, there!"

"Lovely day!" Mom beamed.

"Oh, yes. Lovely."

Billy's father seemed to take the cue. Stepping up onto the board sidewalk, he caught the arm of a man in a group there. "Morning, Stanley!"

The man, round-bellied, turned with a great show of surprise. "Why, hello, Dan! Didn't see you!"

Paw grinned at the other men, his eyes like metal. "Hello, Frank. How are you making it, Archie?"

Because his senses told him things were wrong, Billy tried to pick out the clues that gave him this sensation along his skin. He couldn't see much. He noticed that the smiles on the people's faces seemed strained, and that they glanced at each other, and didn't look his father straight in the eye. They all looked uncomfortable. There was another of those eerie instants of silence, and across the street, where a small band of waddies stood smoking and drinking beer, there was a burst of male laughter that sounded like a thunderclap far in the distance.

"Come, Billy," Mom said, and swept into the front door of Carson's.

Paw, who sometimes was not against slipping away to talk and joke with the men, kept close beside her. Billy followed.

The first step into the big store had been frightening when Billy was younger, and it was still dramatic. The building had a loft, and most of the lower floor was open up to that loft, and there were bins and barrels and boxes everywhere, with all sorts of huge bales and rolls of wire and rope hanging overhead. It was very dark inside, and the effect was of having walked from the normal world into a shadowy cavern peopled by grotesque, shadowy giants. Billy had to pause a moment, and his pores puckered as his other senses drank in impressions: the faint odors of dry rot, dust, hemp, earth, spices, and cloth; the feel of the sawdust floor loose and crumbly underfoot; the mutter of voices and distant chunking of items into sacks. Then his eyes began to adjust and he saw his mother leading the way along to the left, under an enormous down-hanging display of saddles and livery gear, toward the far corner where there were bins and flats containing rolled yard goods.

He hurried to catch up and heard his parents talking.

"They've got no call," his father said bitterly.

"It doesn't matter, Dan," his mother said.

"They're not going to get me in. Not that way or any way—"

"It's all right. It doesn't *matter*."

They walked behind some tall boxes and into the yard goods section. Two housewives were looking at material. Mister Carson himself was cutting from a bolt of calico for another lady. They all looked up as if greatly surprised.

"Hello!" Billy's father said, as if challenging them.

They chimed in with their hellos. One of the women moved away promptly, and the other worked her way to the far end of the tables as Mom began looking at some cloth. Mister Carson was still cutting away at the far table. Billy noticed that his father stood much closer to Mom than he usually did, in public or in private. His father's jaw was set in a hard line.

Mom looked at a tag and murmured in dismay. "It's higher than it was."

"How much higher?" Paw asked.

She showed him the tag. He looked at it.

She said, "We can't afford that, Dan."

"If you need it, you need it."

"If prices go much higher, I don't know—"

Mister Carson came over to face them, his scissors in hand and a measuring tape over his shoulder. "Good morning, folks. How are you today?"

"Fine," Paw said.

"I was noticing this price," Mom said.

"Yes," Carson said cheerfully, "had to raise it some."

Paw said, "Go ahead and get it."

"I don't know," Mom said, looking at the cloth.

"Word with you, Dan?" Carson said.

"Go ahead," Paw said, looking at him.

"Well, maybe it ought to be private."

Paw didn't budge. "Whatever it is, no need to exclude the family, is there?"

Carson looked down at his shoes a moment, seeming flustered. "Well, no, I suppose not—"

"What is it, then?"

Carson looked up at him and seemed to steel himself. "Well, sir, it's about your bill."

69

Mom looked up sharply from the material.

"Our bill?" Paw said, his voice very flat.

"It's—getting on toward fifty dollars again."

"I know what it is, Mister Carson. Exactly."

"Well, I'd appreciate it—if you could see your way clear—"

"Our bill was higher once before," Paw said quietly, his face absolutely flat with what had to be rage. "You know when we'll be able to pay. We've always paid."

"I understand that," Carson said. "Times are hard. But —well, they're hard on businessmen, too." He took a breath. "That's why I've just got to take some—measures."

Paw looked at him. "Meaning?"

Carson put down the scissors and jammed his hands into his apron pockets. "I'm just having to reduce my credit business, folks. That's the short of it."

Mom's hand went up to her throat. "Cash only?"

"That's—the size of it."

The color went down out of Dan Baker's face, and it shocked Billy. He had never known a person's face could get that exact deathly shade. Out of the gray flesh, his father's eyes looked like fire. "Reducing everybody's credit, are you, Mister Carson?"

Carson's hands bulged, as if balling in his apron. "Most."

"Maybe cutting it tighter especially on people who don't sign the pledge, Mister Carson?"

"It's my store, Baker. I run it as I see fit."

Billy's father took a step toward Mister Carson. It was a small step, but Carson moved back. Billy's mother put her hand out and caught his sleeve. "Dan!"

Paw froze, and the look of anguish and anger on his face was something that cut Billy in a way he had never experienced before.

"Dan!" Mom said again. "It's all right. It's all right."

70

Paw whispered, "You can't wait, can you. You can't see that there's an election only two months off."

"We'll solve our problems quicker than that," Carson said.

"You could wait—deal with the problem legally."

"Anything we do will be legal. I've told you that."

"*Rope* legal?"

Carson stiffened. "You're mixing oranges with potatoes, Baker. I came over here to tell you, nicely, that business is bad and I have to reduce credit. I know it's a pinch for you, but that's the way it is until—things change. The other matter has nothing to do with this."

"Maybe you want to pretend that, Carson, but I won't play along."

"Sorry," Carson snapped, and turned to walk away.

Billy's father made a slight, convulsive move. Mom's hand clutched tighter at his arm, holding him back.

"Blast him," Paw whispered. "*Blast* him!"

"*Don't*, Dan," Mom said urgently.

"What can we do without credit? He'd do anything to—"

"Dan," she said softly, tugging at his arm to make him look at her, "it's all right. It's really all right!"

Her eyes were too bright. She was almost, Billy saw with new surprise, about to cry. But she clung to Paw, as if to convince him by her fragile strength alone that it really *was* all right. Was that, Billy wondered, what Moms did? Did they always say it was all right when it wasn't? *Why?*

Billy told McGraw about it in the early evening cool of the mountainside. They squatted on opposite sides of the perch where the old man had put the hawk.

"What did your daddy do then?" McGraw asked. "Did Carson back off?"

"Mister Carson sure didn't back off," Billy told him, "and I guess my paw didn't have much money: all we got was a small bag of salt an' some lye. Paw said we'd just haf to do without some stuff for a while."

McGraw nodded grimly. "He pretty mad, your paw?"

"Was he ever!"

"He think about signing the vigilance pledge, maybe?"

"Heck no! He said if that was how they was gonna act, they could forget him ever signin' anything they might offer him. If they wanted to make it a war on *him*, he told Mister Carson, that was just okay by him."

"Yes," McGraw nodded again. "But the odds aren't very favorable."

"What do you mean?" Billy asked.

"I mean, son, that your father isn't likely to win that kind of a fight. He's got the power of the town against him. And one by one, you mark my words, they'll get his friends away from him—get those other neutral families to sign up to save their credit."

"*They* might sign but *Paw* won't!"

"Might be better off if he would."

"He says he was in a mob once—"

"I know," McGraw sighed wearily. "He's a good man, your daddy. You're lucky, you know that? I sure hate to see a good man getting things turned around where everything is against him like this, though."

"Do you think he should join?" Billy asked.

McGraw grinned, showing a gold tooth in front. "If I had a lot of answers to life's problems, sonny, maybe I wouldn't live on the side of a hill by myself."

It raised the question Billy had been wondering about, and although it was very early in their relationship to ask such a thing, he felt he could trust McGraw, and he blurted it out:

"How come you to live by yourself this way, anyhow?"

McGraw's big jaw set and his eyes became sharp as he

looked hard at Billy. Their glances locked for an instant and Billy had a very strange, very frightening sensation: the feeling that he was looking through McGraw's eyes into an old and private place of pain and regret. *Something* bad had happened to McGraw . . . once, Billy sensed acutely. A bad thing. Like Paw's bad thing with the mob he had seen . . . or been a part of . . . once.

It was startling to know that McGraw, this big, gentle man, also had that kind of bad thing in his past—that it might be so bad that it kept him a recluse on the side of a mountain, shunning all people. Billy simultaneously was fascinated, wanted to know desperately what the secret was, and knew that it was probably a lot better that he didn't know.

McGraw answered his question with the quiet irony of a man who knows he is not to be believed, "I like it alone, sonny. You can see that."

"Aw," Billy growled, embarrassed.

McGraw patted him on the back. "Besides, it keeps me out of troubles like your daddy is in, and it gets me into deals like this one with your hawk. Tell me, don't you figure he looks a little better?"

Billy accepted the change of topic because he had been looking at his hawk all along as they talked, and he was anxious to find out what McGraw thought about it.

The hawk *did* look better, actually sleeker than it had only a day before. It sat its perch strongly, calmly, the hood in place over its eyes. The jesses held its legs in place.

"I thought we might feed him some," McGraw said easily, "then make sure he's calm enough without the hood."

"Do we take the hood off now?" Billy asked eagerly.

McGraw chuckled. "First we take him back in the shed. It's starting to get a little dark now, but let's not have us in a panicked hawk, fighting the jesses like mad and hurting

73

himself. No, we'll take him inside where it's real dim, then we'll gentle him some and remove the hood and see how he does."

Billy nodded and watched McGraw carefully slide his left hand and arm into a stout leather glove and gauntlet, then cautiously move the protected forearm in front of the hooded hawk, nudging its talons and legs. The hawk struggled briefly to keep from being pushed off-balance, backward off the perch, and then saved its balance by stepping up onto the glove. McGraw deftly unhooked the jesses from the swivel that connected to a leather thong on the outdoor perch, twisted the ends of the jesses around his fingers, and led the way to the shed.

Once inside, it took just a minute to install the hawk on its regular perch and get the jesses attached to the new swivel. The shed, with its windows shuttered, was so dark that Billy could scarcely see. McGraw discarded the glove and picked up a long feather, which he used to soothe along the hawk's throat and chest line.

"Gentling him a mite," McGraw explained softly, his voice crooning for the benefit of the hawk.

"Shouldn't you use your fingers?" Billy asked. "Get him used to your touch?"

"Two things wrong with that," McGraw said, his teeth flashing. "One, you might get a little chunk out of your finger. Two—and more important—the oil in your hand would mess up the stuff in his feathers. See, a hawk has natural waterproofing. But your body's oils mess it up. Then if he got out in the weather, in the rain, he wouldn't be able to repel water; he'd get soaked, couldn't fly, would probably die. So you stroke him with a feather when you want to calm him."

Billy pointed to a long, slender stick that McGraw had put beside him. "You use the stick for that, too?"

McGraw made the funny snuffing sound through his nose that Billy had learned was laughter. "Not hardly!"

"What is it for, then?"

"See that can there by the door?"

Billy turned and saw a peach can. "Yessir."

"Bring it over, all right?"

Obeying, Billy saw that the can had several small strips of raw meat in it. The pieces were cut quite small, and lay in a little puddle of blood in the bottom of the can.

As he put the can beside McGraw, he noticed the hawk seem to stir and stiffen, as if catching the scent of the meat.

"Now you just sit back there real easy," McGraw told Billy, his voice crooning for the hawk's benefit, "and don't look right at the hawk if he looks at you. That's important. Hawks are funny. They'll take fright if you stare right at them, sometimes, and no telling how spooky old dimwit here is going to be with the hood off and this much light still left in here."

Billy said nothing. He watched as McGraw, moving very gently and with great precision, untied the little things holding the hood on the hawk's head. He lifted it off. The hawk jerked its head up and looked around. It had a wild, magnificent tilt to its head, and its eyes blazed. Its body trembled. It did not try to fly. Its head turned from side to side, and those blazing eyes gave Billy a deep thrill.

Slowly putting the hood on the floor, McGraw picked up the thin stick. He reached the tip toward the hawk, almost touching the hawk's chest, as he had done with the feather. The hawk moved uneasily on the perch, looking at the tip of the stick.

McGraw touched the hawk with the stick.

The hawk struck down hard with its beak, catching the stick and trying to bite the end off.

McGraw smiled and gentled the stick loose from the

hawk's grasp, and raised it slightly to try to touch the top of the hawk's head. The hawk bitterly snapped at the stick again.

McGraw, with a wink toward Billy, withdrew the stick and reached into the fruit can of raw meat strips. He impaled a tiny strip on the end of the stick and slowly pushed it toward the hawk again. The hawk tilted its head and backed around nervously, trying to figure out the meat. McGraw poked at the hawk. The hawk viciously grabbed the stick. The meat came off in its beak. It chewed and swallowed sharply.

"Good!" McGraw smiled.

"That's how you teach it to eat from you?" Billy guessed.

"It's a real important step," McGraw told him, gently baiting the stick again. "You go from stick to string to lure. If the hawk makes those three transitions, it can be trained pretty well. I'd say this hawk at least is taking to the first step in good shape."

To prove the point, it seemed, the hawk snapped a second strip of raw meat off the stick.

"Good!" McGraw said again, grinning broadly.

A little later, outside, Billy was preparing to head for home. "What's the next step?" he asked McGraw. "I guess we go real slow, huh?"

"The whole training takes just a few weeks, like I think I told you," the older man said. "We make sure he's fixed on the stick, then we go on to the string and then the lure. In the meantime, you know how to carve you a whistle?"

"A whistle?" Billy echoed, puzzled.

McGraw shrugged. "Never mind. I'll fix you one."

"I can do it, if you tell me how you want me—"

"Never mind, never mind. I'll fix it."

"What do I want a whistle for?" Billy asked.

McGraw's eyes twinkled. "At some point, I reckon,

you're going to want to fly this hawk. Right?"

Billy grinned at him. "I ain't going to *want* to, but—"

"I'll accept that. You won't want to, naturally. But you will, because that's what having a hawk is all about, right?"

"Yes, sir, I guess so."

"Okay, you'll need your whistle then."

"You mean to call him back? You mean I blow a whistle and he comes back when he's been flying around? Is that it?"

McGraw's big chest heaved. "Boy, if that hawk takes a mind to just clear out for the tall timber, ain't nothing you or anybody else can do. I mean, you can blow a whistle, jump up and down, ring a cow bell, play a washboard, and stand on your head with your pants falling down, if that hawk wants to *go*, he'll *go*. But a whistle helps sometimes, it's part of the conditioning. So we'll use one. It can't hurt. It might even help."

Billy thought about it. "You'll make me one?"

"I'll make you one," McGraw smiled.

"I'll appreciate it."

"You figure on using this hawk to hunt birds and things for you, Billy?"

"No!" Billy gasped. "I just want to have him—train him."

"Your daddy thinks it's nonsense, eh? Especially with this other trouble?"

"Well, he would," Billy admitted, "if he—" Then he stopped, realizing his mistake.

"If he what?" McGraw asked quickly.

"If he uh, thought about it, or, uh—"

"He doesn't know you brought this hawk up here," McGraw said solemnly.

"No, sir," Billy admitted.

"He doesn't know you've been up here at all."

"No, sir."

77

"What do you suppose he'd think if he knew you were coming up here to see the crazy man?"

"You're not crazy!"

"What would he think?" McGraw persisted gently.

"I don't know," Billy admitted.

"Would he tell you not to come up here any more?"

"No!"

"Are you *sure?*"

"No," Billy admitted.

"I don't want to get you in any trouble, boy," McGraw said sadly.

"I—"

"And I don't want to get me in any trouble, either," the older man added.

"I've asked you for help," Billy pointed out. "It's not like you asked me."

"A lot of folks," McGraw explained, "will be mighty mad at your daddy. They'll blame him for not joining the vigilance committee, and it won't just be because they think everybody ought to band together on a deal like that. They'll be mad at him because he'll be acting *different*—not one of the herd, you see what I mean?"

"Some people oughtn't to be in the herd," Billy said.

McGraw smiled sadly. "The herd seldom thinks so. And that's my point. Just as some folks don't like your daddy for not joining them, why, it's plumb natural for your daddy to distrust *me* some, because I'm a loner, too, right? I don't farm. I don't have a woman. I don't own nothing. There's people that have to be sort of alone, Billy, just like some animals have to go it alone, their own way. Like your hawk. He's that kind. That's why it might be impossible to train him. You never know. But if he goes off his first chance, you can't blame him, that's his nature. And if somebody gets mad at you, or me, for being a little different, why, you

78

can't blame them, either. Folks mistrust folks that are different, especially loners."

"My paw wouldn't mind about me and you and the hawk," Billy said.

McGraw inclined his head at an angle that said he was skeptical. "He's got plenty on his mind without hawk or boy or crazy man trouble, right? If you want to come back, fine. But you make sure you don't get all of us in trouble, or mess up your daddy. Right?"

Billy didn't quite understand, but he nodded agreement.

"Might be some bad times ahead for Springer," McGraw added thoughtfully. "If bad times do come, boy, you just don't worry about this hawk. And you don't worry about me—right?"

"I really don't know what you're talking about now."

"Just promise me," McGraw said sternly.

"I promise," Billy said, confident that he couldn't hurt anything by promising on something he didn't know anything about.

"Better get your rear end home now," McGraw added, swatting him. "Must take you nigh on to an hour to hoof it back and forth."

It took an hour and twenty minutes, but Billy didn't admit it. He shrugged and thanked McGraw rather formally, which brought a smile from the old man, and then he headed home.

He had miscalculated the time slightly, so that night caught him still in the foothills between Springer and his home place. He was still well off from home, as a matter of fact, when he saw the glow of the flames near town, and heard the horsemen coming, and suddenly realized that blind luck had placed him right in the center of something that he wanted no part of whatsoever. He had been walking along the high road that led from town toward the old mine, enjoying the crisp night air and the view, and when the horsemen suddenly exploded out of the night on the road behind him, he only had time to dive behind some rocks as if his life depended on it—which, for all he knew in this moment of shock and terror, it did.

If it had been a lot later at night—if the seeming security of twilight hadn't just faded—he might have been readier for the shock. As it was, one moment he was walking along the ridge road, enjoying the view of open land and mountains and clutter of town well off to the north, and then the next instant he had first spotted the glow of flames south of the town, and before he could even begin to guess whose spread it might be on fire, the crash of all the horses was coming up the road and was upon him.

He darted off the road and hit the erosion ditch, rolling between boulders and jagged rocks still hot from the day's sunlight. Dust exploded over his hiding place as the horses pounded past, some astonishingly close. In the starlight he had the impression there were about two dozen riders, and the clatter of hooves, groaning of saddle leather, and clink of metal were tremendous.

The horsemen were not, however, going by. They were reining up, pinwheeling, bumping into each other, and yelling hoarse instructions as they got to a stop and tried to get some semblance of organization. The dust thickened, choking Billy's throat and nostrils. This was when he saw that most of the riders were masked—their heads covered with sacklike hoods that allowed only pale eyeholes for vision. They looked—*unworldly,* really eerie, under the hoods. All were heavily armed, and in the center of the melee were four riders without hoods: young men, strangers, hatless, their clothing in shreds, faces hideous with blood, tied in

80

their saddles and reeling like grotesque rag dolls as their frightened mounts pivoted and wheeled, badly controlled by the hooded men who were fighting their own excited horses at the same time they tried to control the reins of those with men tied to their saddles.

"All right!" a man bellowed hoarsely, swinging his horse around in a circle near the center of the roadway. "Line 'em up there!"

Was the voice familiar? In his hiding place, Billy dared only a peek through the rocks. The man was thick-set, strong. His voice sounded like one Billy knew. It was darker, however, with an excitement and passion, and maybe, Billy thought, he was wrong—

"We'll go right through here!" another man yelled excitedly, pointing to the line of wind-blasted cottonwoods lining the road on the far side.

"Swing 'em around!" the first man ordered. "And get them new ropes up over the branches there; let's not drag this out!"

Arms swung and ropes snaked up and over branches. Watching, Billy saw with horror exactly what was going to take place. This high road, this spot of rock and wind-blasted old trees, could be seen for miles in all directions during the daytime hours. The prisoners, their faces ghastly with fear of what they saw coming, were going to be strung up for all to see tomorrow—and as long as their bodies remained in a piece?

"Make a noose," the big man who was the leader yelled, swinging out of his saddle. "That's it. Somebody get some of those torches going. Set a guard back down the road, there, Harvey! Hurry it up! Hurry it up!"

Everything was already a hurry, and a confusion. Horses bounced into one another, horsemen cursed and muttered and maneuvered, the ropes were over the limbs and riders leaned close, fashioning big, hideous nooses, and the four prisoners were encircled, tied helpless to their saddles. Several horsemen held them closely guarded with rifles leveled across pommels. The faces of the captives seemed to glow with an unearthly pallor, but in the dust and crimson smoke of newly lighted torches Billy could not make out any expressions.

"Shove them into line, there, and get the ropes on!" the leader ordered.

The hooded horsemen forced the prisoners' horses together, lining them roughly under the trees, pressing them forward so that the nooses hung down across their faces. One of the prisoners brushed against the heavy rope, uttered a strangled cry, and started to fall sideways, unconscious, in the saddle. Hands shot out and held him upright.

"All right!" the leader shouted.

The hooded riders stilled. The horses were controlled. The prisoners stared, haggard with the gaunt pallor of doomed men, as the hooded leader strode across the roadway to face the line of men and horses under the nooses in the trees.

The lights from a half-dozen torches cast crimson-yellow shimmerations. Smoke curled redly against flames. It was, for an instant, very still, and Billy watched between the boulders, his heart hammering.

"We've burned your squatter shacks," the hooded leader said. "We've brought you here. We are the new law in Springer. No deputies, no long hearings, no paroles, no juries, no delays, no loopholes, no weakness! These are our homes and our fields and our people, and we're together!

"You're just some of the new people who have come in here. You drink, you gamble, you cheat, you steal, you insult our women and scandalize our young people, you make nothing, you want to take it all."

The leader paused again, and his hooded figure seemed to swell with a deep breath. "You four stole food tonight. You broke into a store. You were followed. Your guilt was judged by us, the vigilance committee. We can set our own penalties; it's our land, our law. We could set an example of you, warn the others."

He paused again, and the sparks and hissing of smoke from torches was the only sound in the vast, nightmare night.

"We can hang you now, until you are dead, and leave you here to show we mean business."

One of the prisoners moaned.

Billy, watching, tried to think of a way to escape. He didn't want to see this.

"We aren't going to hang you," the leader went on, his voice booming in the stillness. "We could. We choose not to—*this* time. You're to go. Each of you. Warn the others like you. Let them know the vigilance committee is organized. We are ready. We are giving this one warning. There will be no more warnings. We want no bloodshed, but we're going to protect our homes and families."

Then, before Billy could quite comprehend it, the leader made a slashing motion with his empty hand. From all sides of the prisoners, knives appeared and sliced through ropes that held them. One of the prisoners, deprived of support, keeled out of the saddle and hit the earth like a half-empty sack of feed.

The hooded leader swung into his saddle. His companions followed suit. Dust exploded from the roadway. They started back the way they had come, moving past one another in a chaotic rush.

Grabbing the chance, Billy scrambled through the boulders and along the edges of the ditch, down the weedy field on the far side, heading downhill and in the general direction of home as fast as he could go.

Partway down the hill, in the greeny-wet meadow, he rolled over to rest, and looked back up the hill toward the spot where he had almost been caught.

One or two of the torches had been dropped on the roadway, and it cast an eerie pinkish light against pluming smoke and the undersides of trees along the road, where the nooses hung. Two of the prisoners sat in their saddles, perfectly still, heads down, as if still stunned. One was out of sight, his horse standing riderless, and Billy knew he was the one who had fallen to the ground. The fourth man stood beside his horse, arms hanging limp, head down, utterly exhausted, shocked, unmoving as the pink smoke of the torches drifted about him and into the black night sky.

Far off toward Springer, in the valley, the glow of the answering fire, the one that had burned them out, was now a dull coal.

Billy hurried on toward home, and when he saw the pale lights of the windows of his own house, he felt a relief so intense it was painful. The war in the valley, he knew without doubt, was now on. But at least tonight his father had been allowed to remain a neutral. Tomorrow—nobody could guess about tomorrow.

Six

On the morning after the first strike by the vigilance committee, Billy's father had visitors again. This time it was two men who farmed on the far side of Springer; their names were Judkins, a lank, dour man with a jaw misshapen by a wad of tobacco, and Braithwaite, an older man whose very sap seemed to have been drained and dried away by the struggle of making a living on the soil. Billy's father invited them to climb down off their wagon and come in, but they seemed reluctant to go near his house; they stood uneasily by the scant patch of shade thrown by the swing tree.

"I guess you heard about the action last night?" Judkins asked, shifting his tobacco wad.

Dan Baker leaned on his shovel and looked angry but controlled. "Somebody came by, told me enough."

Judkins spat. "Vigilance committee."

"I assumed that."

"Nobody hurt, but those boys ain't around today."

"I see."

Braithwaite removed his broad-brimmed hat and mopped his forehead. "Some of the neighbors around here, seeing

85

how the committee got something done, joined right up this morning."

"Is that so?"

"Yep. Sleds, down the road there a piece, for example. They joined up this morning, first thing."

"I guess they needed their credit," Dan Baker said sharply.

"I'd say more likely they saw what has to be done for the common good," Braithwaite said.

"What do you want with me?"

Judkins raised his eyebrows, as if offended. "Just paying our respects. The vigilance committee wants to make sure that each and every citizen, whether he happens to be a member or not, understands what's going on, what actions are taken, what's at stake. The committee doesn't do anything without approval of its members and the people it protects."

"I see."

"You changed your mind about joining?" Judkins asked bluntly.

"No."

"How about your obligation to your family? Look at this boy, here." Judkins inclined his head toward Billy, who stood silent by the fence. "Don't you think you got an obligation to him?"

"Thanks for telling me my obligations as a father," Dan Baker said. "I really appreciate it, gentlemen."

After the two visitors had been gone a short time, Billy was down by the barn when a visitor of his own appeared. Jeremy Sled looked a little sheepish as he squatted against the barn wall and watched Billy plait leather for the reins.

"What's the matter?" Billy asked him.

Jeremy Sled looked at his splayed bare toes stretched out in front of him. "Those guys come to yur house this morning too?"

"Yep."

"Yur daddy join this time?"

"Nope."

"Mine did."

"Yep, that's what they said."

"He had to, Billy," Jeremy said quickly.

Billy was stunned at his friend's reaction. "You act *embarrassed* that he joined! It ain't like joining was *bad*. I wish *my* paw would join!"

"My daddy joined for the credit at the store. He called it caving in."

That concept startled Billy, too. "I dunno if that's what it was. The vigilantes might do bad stuff—but maybe it has to be done."

"If it was a good bunch of people, would they hold up your credit to make you join?"

"I hadn't thought of that exactly that way," Billy admitted lamely.

Jeremy sighed. "Well, tell me about your hawk."

"He's fine," Billy said, glad to change the subject.

"And the crazy man?"

"He ain't crazy, Jeremy. His name is McGraw, and he's real nice."

"What did you say when you first got there? How does he look? Was he mean at first? What's he done to the hawk so far? How bad hurt was it? What do you plan to do next? You been back since you took the hawk up there? How long does it take to get there? Could I go with you?"

"I don't see why you couldn't," Billy said, answering the last question first. "And the hawk's okay, he's fine. We're going to train him. We've started already. We've made jesses."

"What are jesses?"

Billy felt pleasantly superior. "I'll show you when we get there."

"You mean you will take me?"

"I don't see why not."

"Boy, howdy! I'll be sure and not tell my daddy!"

"Why not?" Billy demanded. "I mean, you don't have to hide it from him, you know."

"Well, have you told *yours?*"

"No," Billy admitted.

"Well, then?"

"I don't think he'd really care too much about the hawk being at Mister McGraw's. It's just that he told me, Paw did, not to mess with any more animals."

"My daddy would be mad about that old man."

"I don't know why."

"Because he's different, Billy."

"The old man is?"

"Sure."

"Well, yes. But he ain't crazy."

"My daddy says, don't mess with people that are different from you."

"*Why?*"

Jeremy hesitated. "Well—don't take no chances, he says."

They talked about it some more. When Jeremy finally left, he came right out and admitted that he might like to meet McGraw, Daddy's objections or no. Billy said he would see if McGraw minded having another visitor.

The whole idea of hiding his actions from Paw—and possibly gaining Jeremy as a coconspirator—continued to bother Billy. But even with all the trouble building in town, he found he was getting more and more preoccupied with the hawk and more and more pleased with McGraw and the project and getting the hawk manned.

That, McGraw said, was what you called the first stages

88

of training a hawk. You manned him. Some hawks would never accept manning. They fought and fought, and just beat themselves to death, fighting the jesses, or they starved themselves to death by refusing to eat. Billy had said this made hawks seem real dumb, but McGraw had countered that it only proved that hawks had a tremendous amount of spirit. It was no mean trick to man a hawk, he said, because hawks had to agree to it, sort of, and that meant building trust and confidence between a person and a wild thing—a creature that would never really be tame in the way dogs became tame, or even cats.

"There are grown men that would give anything to man a hawk, sonny," McGraw had explained while they watched the bird sit its perch under the hood. "That's because it takes a special kind of man . . . or boy. You see, the hawk has senses we don't even know about yet. Just look at your hawk, there. He knows we're here. He's listening. He's *feeling* you, right now, this instant. He's beginning to know you. He's making up his mind. You've got some advantages; he's never really been loose in the wild, and you saved his life. So he ought to train a little easier. But if you aren't the right kind of person underneath—if he can't *feel* you're right, in his heart—then there's no way he'll ever train for you."

"Do you think he knows I saved his life?" Billy asked.

"Ah, he knows, sonny."

"How?"

"He *knows.*"

It was a mysterious, almost frightening thing, but Billy knew it was true. People said he had a way with animals, and he knew he understood Alexander the Great, for example, far better than most folks would have. But McGraw's words went deep into him, because the way the old man

89

spoke was clear evidence that hawks were not just another kind of wild creature. They were special.

Billy had already sensed this, but it was becoming clearer all the time.

Even before saving the hawk's life, he had often imagined what it must be like, having wings and those keen, keen eyes, and being able to soar; it was a very special existence. How could you ever be sure what a hawk might think, or what it could know? And now McGraw said some hawks would simply die rather than accept manning. Thinking about it, Billy no longer saw this as dumb, but as noble.

"Do you suppose," he had asked McGraw, "we could unhood him now?"

McGraw thought about it, rubbing his lips with his stubby fingers. "It's fairly dark and he seems quiet. Of course, it's early to be trying it yet. You know what happened the last time."

The last time they had unhooded the hawk very carefully, being cautious not to stare into those wide, unblinking yellow eyes. The hawk had held its perch in perfect silence and stillness for almost a minute. Then it had exploded into violent motion, trying to fly. Its wings, almost a yard broad, had beaten the air, and it had hit the end of the leash line and fallen into the dirt, its wings continuing to thrash with a terrible urgency.

It had scared Billy a little, and McGraw had been forced to replace the hood. There were, McGraw had said after the commotion died down, good days and bad days.

Now, however, Billy felt this brimming impulse to try again—now, even though it was late and it had not been planned. He knew the chance they were running.

"Let's try," he said.

McGraw nodded.

Gently, making no undue sound, the old man moved

90

around the hawk's perch. He made sure, without touching them, that the jesses and swivels were securely affixed. He looped the leash line out to prevent knots. Then, using one hand in that amazingly dexterous fashion of his, he untied the leather hood and flipped it back off the hawk's head.

The hawk's feathers spread out, magically, as if some new inner fire had suddenly swollen from within. The size of the bird seemed to double, and it trembled, moving slightly on the perch. Its head turned ever so slightly— toward Billy.

Billy looked away, but kept the hawk in his peripheral vision. His heart thumped. He knew the hawk was about to burst into attempted flight, and then there would be that awful beating of the wings against the ground again.

The hawk partially spread its wings, allowing them to unfold and droop downward. It froze in that position. It seemed to be a statue. There was a breath of wind, but the hawk paid no attention. Its eyes focused on Billy, dilating slightly, focusing with an intensity he could only imagine. The hawk was looking not only at him but *into* him, he sensed, filtering out false impressions, picking out those things that were true from those that were only illusion.

The hawk did not attempt to fly.

"Maybe it'll be all right," Billy said softly.

"I guess that's a hopeful sign, anyway," McGraw agreed.

"Am I good enough?" Billy asked impulsively. "Am I good enough *inside*, I mean?"

"I hope so, sonny," McGraw replied. "That's what we're gonna find out, though, isn't it."

In the afternoon, Billy's mother was at the Sleds', quilting, and Paw was off in the gullies somewhere, looking for a cow. That was when Sheriff Ad Sweeney came.

Sweeney was enormously fat. There was no mistaking

him. He liked to tell people that he knew he didn't *look* like a lawman, which was an indirect way of also saying that he was a pretty good one, despite the looks.

"Your daddy here, sonny?" he panted, riding up on his sway-backed gelding.

"No sir," Billy told him. "But he ought to be back soon."

"I'm Ad Sweeney," the sheriff said, swinging out of the saddle. "I'm sheriff around here. Course I know I don't look much like a sheriff, but I am, by grannies."

Billy grinned manfully and stuck out a hand for a shake. This gave him an instant to study Ad Sweeney, who was about five feet, eight inches tall, about four feet, six inches wide, and as bald as a billard ball. Sheriff Ad Sweeney wore pants that looked like circus tents, and a coat that had to have taken a whole bale of cotton just to manufacture it. He wore a beaded-brim sombrero, pale blue shirt, and big silver spurs on his boots, which looked like Size 14 triple wide. He looked like a tall man who had gotten squashed by some tragic and inexorable accidental force applied directly to the top of his head. He wore a sixgun, all right, and shells and a badge on his suit collar, but he looked like a disaster waiting to happen. An enemy wouldn't have needed to aim to shoot him; all he would have needed was a range within a mile plus a general compass heading. No wonder the horse was sway-backed. The miracle was that it was still alive.

"Heard your daddy was one that wouldn't join the vigilance bunch," Ad Sweeney said, leaning against the fence post, which creaked.

"You heard right," Billy told him.

Sweeney inserted a quarter of a pound of chewing plug into his mouth. "How come?"

"He told them he don't like mobs."

Sweeney digested this. "They've cut off his credit."

92

"Yes, sir."

"Given him a bad time."

"Yes, sir."

"He hasn't give in."

"Heck, no! Are you kidding!"

"I'd like to talk to him. How long you figure it will be before he gets back?"

"Well, I dunno, maybe another hour or two."

Sweeney spat. "Not good enough. I got to go to town. Tell you what: How about you telling him I was by, and if he could come to Springer for a talk, I'd be mighty appreciative."

"Are you gonna be around town for a while?" Billy asked, knowing it was an impudent question.

"Guess so," Sweeney sighed, rubbing his enormous belly.

"Well, I'll sure be glad to tell my paw you was by."

"Tell him I do need to talk to him, you hear?"

"Yes, sir, I will."

"People that stand for regular law and order have to get together . . . now," Sweeney muttered somberly.

"Because of last night, you mean?"

"Naw," Sweeney said, and swung up into the saddle of the poor horse, which positively staggered under the crushing weight. "After this afternoon."

"I didn't figure anything could happen this afternoon to make it worse than what it was last night, boy!"

Sweeney looked down at him, and the sheriff's pudgy face was slack and gray with tension of the sort one did not ordinarily expect to find, somehow, in the expression of a fat man. A fat man was supposed to be jolly.

"You don't know about poor old Plotford, then," he said.

Billy remembered that Plotford was the area deputy. "No, sir. What happened?"

"What happened," Sweeney said, "was six bullets in the back, from close range."

"Aw!"

"'Aw' is right," Sweeney said somberly. "About all the good a man is, after that much lead being pumped into him, is if you got a lake or a river nearby, and you need a boat anchor."

Billy stared up at the fat man, and he was fighting to get it figured out in ways that made sense. The vigilantes had struck, and somebody had struck back—at Plotford. And now Sweeney was here, back to the wall. Calling on Billy's paw. *Why?*

"You looking for help, Sheriff Sweeney?" he asked.

Sweeney shrugged, but said nothing.

"You're not thinking of asking *my paw!*"

"You just give him my message, right, boy? And tell him I'd sure admire to see him before nightfall, for a friendly talk." Sweeney's enormous torso heaved again in another sigh. "Seems like a lot of stuff happens around here after nightfall these days, don't it. So we better be sure to meet before."

"I'll tell him, Sheriff."

Sweeney, slumped in the saddle as if he carried the weight of the world, rode away.

Billy turned back toward his house in time to see his mother come out onto the porch and signal for him to come over to her.

"What was that all about?" she asked, worried.

He told her what Sweeney had said. As he got to the part about Deputy Plotford, she stiffened, looked off into the distance, and twisted her jaw as if in suppressed pain.

"Dan was right," she said. "This is how it goes. Now the sheriff will try to hire more men, the vigilantes will strike back blindly, the others will counterattack—" She paused,

94

took a breath, slipped her arm around his shoulders, and squeezed him, hard. "I want you to stay close to home, Billy. You have to be careful. We all do."

Billy thought about McGraw and the hawk and how far he had to trek to get to them each evening. He had already had one close call, which he was not about to tell *anyone*. There was no way to know what someone might do if they found out he had observed the hooded men on the hill road—and had recognized at least the voices of Carson and two of his close friends. He had to be awfully careful or his visits to the mountain might be cut off for any one of several reasons.

That was something he couldn't allow to happen, he thought. Maybe it was silly to be so caught up in this whole hawk business when so much else was going wrong, when his paw was in trouble. But the hawk *was* important. Sometimes when he was away from it, he almost had a hard time remembering why it was so important. But it was. He knew that he wasn't going to have too many years left when he could have something like the hawk, something to depend on and try to improve and take care of. Maybe the hawk was the last real pet he would *ever* have. And the hawk wouldn't have been alive at all if it hadn't been for him. Now it was up to him—to him and McGraw—to make the hawk into a trained hunter, sort of a *completed* hawk.

"Your father will probably want to take you into Springer with him when he goes," Billy's mother told him now, worriedly. "So if you have any chores, or any of your traps to check, you'd better go ahead and do it so you'll be ready when he gets back."

"Do you think the sheriff is gonna ask Paw to be a deputy?" Billy asked.

Her face drew together and revealed a dozen fine lines of worry that he had never seen before. "I don't know."

Billy stared at her and had the feeling of things closing in upon them both. If Paw became a deputy, he became like Plotford, and Plotford was—

"Do your chores," his mother reminded him again, breaking his train of thought.

Given the circumstances, Billy figured his chances of seeing McGraw and his hawk today had now vanished. He didn't have time to get to the mountain and back in time to meet his father, and the trip to Springer would probably make it too late for him to start when they got back. He went out to the pet pens, fed and watered everybody, picked some ticks off Alexander the Great, and hoed the corn patch a little. Luckily for the sake of his back, his father came back with the stray cow before there was time to do more than a dozen hills in the corn patch. Billy told him the story given him by Sheriff Sweeney. Paw looked grim, and said he would go in to town. He told Billy he would appreciate some company. Right, Billy said. They left.

A stranger, Billy thought, could have told instantly that something was badly wrong in the town of Springer.

The funny thing was that specifics were so hard to pin down. Riding in with his father on the front bench of the wagon, he knew at once. But how? He tried to figure it out, and it wasn't easy to pin down.

Horses stood at racks along the broad main street, as always, and a couple of wagons were at Carson's for loading. Down by the city building the flag was whipping in a stiff afternoon breeze. Bright white clouds drifted against a painfully blue sky behind the mountains to the north and east. A couple of lazy hounds snoozed in front of the jail-

96

house. Off on the side streets, beneath trees, little kids played and chased each other. A couple of the old-timers sat on the iron bench in front of the small black metal fence around the old cannon in the square. Dust skittered along. A crew of men was digging a ditch for drainage or something beside the livery barn.

Everything normal.

But not really.

The only thing Billy could put his finger on was the lack of movement along the street. There were no horsemen drifting along, as there usually were, and none of the usual loungers along the fronts of any of the saloons on the far side of the square. As a matter of fact, most of the saloons looked closed. It was a little like an election day, where everything looked fine on the outside, but anything really going on was going on behind doors or curtains someplace. Billy thought of the hooded men of last night, and he didn't like it. It didn't seem right, them being hooded that way, hidden and violent by night, just as hidden—but behind a veneer of business respectability—by day. He wondered what they would look and feel like out here now, with their hoods.

His father drove the wagon to the jail and reined up on its shady side. As he started to get down, the jailhouse door opened and Sheriff Sweeney strode out. He had stripped off his shirt, so now he wore only his long-sleeved underwear top. It made him look even fatter.

"Dan!" he said with grim pleasure. "Thanks for coming in!"

"Come on, boy," Dan Baker told Billy.

"Can we, uh, talk without the boy?" Sweeney asked diffidently.

Dan Baker hesitated.

"I'd just as soon set here in the shade anyhow, Paw," Billy told him.

97

Baker nodded and went into the jail with Sweeney.

Settling down against some wadded feed sacks, Billy watched some distant birds fly, and thought about his hawk and then about the town's troubles. It was hard to believe that there was any trouble *right now*. Along the row of saloons where the rowdiest waddies usually hung out, there was some laughter from inside and the clatter of a piano somewhere. But there wasn't anything bad going on. It seemed hard to believe, from the peaceful look of things now, that violence walked in the night.

Billy was sitting there, thinking about it, when he heard a faint tinkling sound, a little like a muffled cowbell. It seemed to be coming from the street behind him. He turned.

Coming up the street slowly was a big man, grizzled and overweight, some, wearing raggy clothes and carrying a crooked walking stick cut from a tree limb. He had a floppy black felt hat and floppy brown leather boots, probably made from deer hide, by his own hand, and he was leading a pack mule that was about the sorriest creature Billy had ever seen. The old man slumped along steadily, at a ground-eating gait, minding his own business.

"Hey, Mister McGraw!" Billy called delightedly.

The old man paused in midstride and looked up sharply. It took him a second to spot Billy. Then his grin shone. He waved his free hand in a slow salute. "Hello, young feller!"

"What're you doing?" Billy asked.

McGraw slumped over, leading the sleepy mule, and leaned thankfully on the front wheel of the wagon. "Well, sir, even the old crazy man of the hill has to get a few supplies now and then. I needed a little salt, some string, a couple of swivels. Might even splurge and get me some canned tomatoes and a touch of sugar and spice." McGraw winked. "Just for snakebite, naturally."

"Naturally."

"What brings you to town, anyhow? You buying some whiskey, too?"

"Aw, my paw's inside, talking to the sheriff."

McGraw sobered. "Sheriff's honoring Springer with his presence, eh?"

"He sure is. And last night his deputy got killed."

McGraw jerked. "Killed! Poor old Plotford?"

"Yes, sir."

McGraw sighed and shook his head sadly. "He was a good man. I knew him a little. We'd met. He didn't try to run me off, like some lawmen would. We talked about fishing. He liked fishing. Never had much luck, though, he said." McGraw tipped his hat back and scratched his head. "Guess his luck is *all* run out, now."

"I don't know how long my paw will be talking in here," Billy said, "but it looks like I won't be making it up to see you and the hawk later today."

McGraw shrugged. "Everything's going fine. No need to worry about the hawk, anyhow."

"Do you think his wing is looking better?"

"Aw, say, his wing is going to be just fine! And I had him on the glove today, walking him around the darkened shed without the hood, just to get him started on being used to that, and he grabbed me real good with *both* sets of talons. I'd say he's coming around just real fine."

Billy felt a chill of pleasure. "What do we do next for training him?"

"Well, sir, of course we keep adding light, getting him used to being carried and handled, and we'll be making his food bigger, you know, so he has to learn to tear it apart with his beak and his back talons the way he would in nature. Then, after a few days of that kind of stuff, we can—"

"What are you doing there, mister?"

The voice was so close and so unexpected that both McGraw and Billy turned to face it in the same instant that it interrupted what had been their quiet conversation.

Standing by the back corner of the jail building, his butcher's apron around his ample middle, stood a man Billy knew only as Chafflin. He was medium height, heavy-set, bald, about fifty. He had small, close-set eyes, and the only time Billy had ever seen him before, those eyes had been jolly. They were anything but jolly now; they looked angry, sullen, and perhaps a trifle scared. Billy saw, with a shock, that Chafflin had a revolver belted around his round middle under the blood-stained apron.

McGraw looked puzzled. "You talking to us, mister?"

"What are you doing to that boy?" Chafflin demanded.

McGraw smiled slowly. "We're just passing the time of day, friend."

"What's your business here?"

"I live here," McGraw said, his voice going softer, disappointed and guarded now. He pointed toward the mountains. "Up there."

Chafflin's eyes widened. "You're the crazy man."

"He's not crazy!" Billy protested.

"You better be quiet, boy," Chafflin growled.

"That's what you think!" Billy shot back. "He's my friend and we're talking, and you better butt out, mister!"

"Boy," Chafflin said, moving a step closer, "you need some manners."

"Don't bother him," McGraw said with a sudden new sharpness in his tone.

Chafflin paused, looked from Billy to McGraw and then back again, and lowered his eyes for an instant. He was clearly uncertain about how he should proceed. He took a breath and started again.

"I'm a member of the vigilance committee," he an-

100

nounced stiffly. "Our pledge is law and order, and people living together so as not to bother each other. I aim to uphold that pledge."

"What law were we breaking?" McGraw asked.

"You don't belong here. You've got no legitimate business in town. There's no reason for you to be bothering this boy. I saw you from my shop and I'm checking you out."

"Friend, I'm not bothering this boy."

"You don't belong here. Move along."

"Who decided I don't belong here?"

Chafflin looked puzzled.

McGraw pressed the point. "Is there a list of people that belong here? Am I the wrong size or color to belong here? Funny. I thought only Negroes weren't allowed in Springer."

Whether Chafflin would have responded directly, Billy would never know; for at that moment there was a sound behind him, on the porch of the jail. Chafflin glanced up and immediately began smoothing his hands on his apron in a nervous way.

Billy turned.

Sweeney was on the porch. "Well, now, let's not have any fuss here, shall we?" He was smiling.

Behind Sweeney stood Billy's father. He looked unhappy. He had a deputy's badge pinned on his shirt.

Seven

"I didn't want it and I'm not qualified for it," Billy's father said doggedly at the supper table that night. "Maybe I don't even have a right to take the risk, with you and Billy to watch after. But it's all getting out of hand. Sweeney has to have support. No one is going to be safe unless it's stopped right now."

Seated in front of a plate of food she hadn't touched, Billy's mother had never looked any more solemn or worried. She looked first at Billy, then at her husband. "I know you had to accept it, dear."

"It's not a matter of keeping regular duty. All I really have to do is *be* here—in this part of the county—and keep Sweeney informed. There has to be a—a representative of the real law, you see?"

Ellen Baker nodded, her face averted.

Billy's father turned to him. "I meant to ask you earlier, but now is as good a time as any. Who was that old man you were with when I came back out of the jail?"

"That was Mister McGraw," Billy told him, worried.

"I got the feeling there was bad blood between him and Chafflin."

"No bad blood," Billy corrected. "We was talking, and old Chafflin came over and butted in."

"Billy," his mother said, reproving him.

"Well, it's true!"

Dan Baker shook his head. "Some of the roughest element got the word real fast. Some are already gone. But it won't stop now. Chafflin and the others like him will use the committee to try to drive out everyone who isn't exactly what they want, and pretty soon the law will have nothing to do with who's getting bothered."

Billy thought about it and didn't say anything.

"What were you doing with this man McGraw, anyway? Who is he?"

"He's sort of a friend of mine," Billy hedged.

"A friend? Where did you meet?"

"Well—at his place."

"Where does he live?"

"Sort of, uh, out."

"Who is he, Billy?" Paw asked sternly.

"Well," Billy said, giving up, "he lives up in the mountains."

"Is he the *crazy man?*"

"He ain't crazy, Paw!"

"I know, I know. But—is he the one people *call* the crazy man?"

"I guess some people call him that."

"How did you two meet?" Paw demanded.

"Well," Billy said slowly, feeling trapped, "I had this animal that was hurt."

"What kind of an animal?"

"A hawk."

"One of those hawks you were talking about a few weeks ago," Paw guessed.

"Yes, sir, and one of 'em fell and got hurt, and I knew

103

I couldn't bring it home because of what you'd said about no more animals, but I couldn't just let it die, and Jeremy mentioned the crazy man. I went to him and he took the hawk for me. He's not crazy at all, Paw! You saw him today. He's fine. He's a nice man. He knows all about hawks, too, and we're training my hawk. It's getting all better, and it already wears a hood and eats meat you give it on a stick, and tomorrow or the next day we'll start it learning to be carried around on my fist without the hood and then we teach it to eat meat in chunks and then—"

"Are you still that much of a baby?" Paw snapped.

"Huh?" Billy looked up and saw his father's face contorted with frustration and anger.

"When are you going to start growing up, boy?"

"What are you *mad* about? Just because I've got me a hawk—"

Paw threw up his hands. "The town is torn to pieces, the valley is going up in smoke, a deputy is dead and I'm forced to take his place in title at least, the vigilance committee cuts off our credit to force us out, the rough element would probably like to see me dead—and *you're* out playing with a hawk!"

Billy's mother stirred. "Dan," she said. Soft reproof in her tone.

"No!" Paw retorted. "When is he going to start accepting responsibility?"

The anger in Billy was like the flash of sunlight from a mirror. "When are *you?*" he shot back.

"What?" Paw said, startled.

"When are you going to join the vigilance committee so you can help get something done around here?" Billy demanded.

"I told you why, Billy. Now—"

"I know they're rough," Billy groaned. "I know the stuff

104

they do isn't the neatest. But they're getting the job done, right? So what can be so wrong?"

"That's like saying anything that meets the ends is all right," Paw told him. "That's like saying if I want to butcher a pig, I can go out and shoot it full of buckshot to kill it, since all that matters is getting it dead."

Billy shook his head. "You told me to try to grow up, Paw, and I ain't very big or smart. But that kind of stuff has nothing to do with what we're talking about. I'm big enough to know that much."

His father's eyes narrowed with pain. "What is the issue, then, boy?"

"You tell me to take responsibility—but you don't."

"I've told you why I'm against mob action!"

"Is that it, Paw—or is it just a way to hide?"

"I've heard all I'm going to hear on that line," Paw said hoarsely. He was shaking. "You'll do as I say, young man. Do you hear me?"

"Yes, sir," Billy choked, afraid he was going to blubber.

"You're going to start learning to be a man. When you're a child, you act as a child. Now you're becoming a man. You have to put away the things of a child."

Billy, staring through blurred eyes, said nothing.

Paw pointed at him. "If you won't grow up on your own accord, I'll make you grow up."

"Now, Dan," Mom said tensely, watching from the side with her hands knotted.

"You stay out of it," Paw snapped. "It's between him and me. He has to learn responsibility. He can't be sneaking off across the mountain to play with some old fool and some stupid bird every day when we have all this trouble. It's out of the question!" He turned to Billy, his face tight with anger. "Now listen to me. You are not to go see that old man again. Not under any circumstances."

"Dan!" Mom gasped.

"For all you can tell," Paw went on, goaded, "they'll turn on *him,* next. He's different too, you know. They could get on him. Then where would that put you, and the rest of us? You'll just have to stay away from him."

"What about *my hawk?"* Billy asked.

"I told you you weren't going to have a hawk. You're not going to have one. Forget it."

Billy looked at his father, then at his mother, and he was thinking of what he had to say to make them change their minds somehow. One moment he thought he had everything under control, and then, in the next instant, shockingly, he was crying. It was awful—he had thought he would never get caught crying like this again. The tears seemed to spurt from his eyes and splash all down his cheeks and chin. He saw his father's face go slack with astonishment.

Billy said, "I'm *not* going to forget it, Paw!"

"You *what?"*

"I'm not hurting anything going to see Mister McGraw and my hawk. I'm doing all my chores and anything else you tell me. You—you got no right, telling me to stop doing something that isn't even bad."

"We'll see about that," Paw snapped, starting to leave his chair.

"Dan!" Ellen Baker's voice was very sharp.

Dan Baker glanced at her and paused.

"Leave the boy alone," she said softly, with great firmness.

"He shouldn't be playing around. He has to grow up. It might even be dangerous—"

"Dan, I want you to leave the boy alone. Let him have his trips to work with that hawk, if that's what he wants."

Paw's face was cloudy. "You'd cross me on this?"

106

Billy had never seen his mother's expression as hard, or as serene. Her tone was velvet. "I want you to let him be on this, Dan. Don't make that sound like I'm crossing you. But when you're wrong, you're wrong—and someone has to make you see it."

"You're challenging my authority over my own son! And over a stupid hawk!"

"I seldom question you, Dan. You know that. And if the issue is so small, then let me have my way on it. Let Billy have his hawk, and go see that old man, if it means so much to him."

"I never thought you'd cross me this way about my own son!"

"He's my son too."

Fascinated, Billy watched his father stare a long time, in silence, at his mother. His father's face worked, and a lot of things were almost said, but got held back, and the struggle showed in the muscles of his face. He was on his feet, Paw was, and he towered over Billy's mother. But the way she stood, slender and straight and so *calm,* made it seem as if she were surrounded by an invisible wall of protective quiet and strength.

"All right!" Dan Baker shouted finally, throwing up his hands. "All *right!* If that's what you both want, go ahead!" He whirled on Billy. "Your trips up there will be on your own time, though, boy, and don't forget that! No shirking of chores! No excuses! And remember, I didn't want you to do any of it!"

Before Billy could reply, his father had turned and stormed out of the house.

The door slammed behind him, shaking pans hanging on the wall.

Billy's mother raised her eyebrows and began cleaning off the supper table.

107

"He's really, really mad," Billy breathed.

"He has a lot on his mind," Mom said quietly.

"He—with him being a deputy and all, maybe I ought not to go to the mountain, after all."

She turned to look at him with eyes he could not read. "It means a lot to you, doesn't it."

"Oh, *yes*," he admitted with a burst of candor that was rare between the two of them. "I've always wanted a hawk. And McGraw—he's a nice man, I think maybe even he's lonesome, you know, because he always likes to see me, and we talk about stuff—"

"Then go when you can," his mother told him calmly. "You'll lose your last chances to play—and laugh—soon enough, God knows."

"But I hate for Paw to be so mad."

"Your father is under a terrible strain. But as for being mad at either of us, you or me—" she paused and smiled a secret little smile—"he'll get over that, darling. A man doesn't stay angry with his woman very long. You'll learn that one day."

"He can stay mad at *me*, though," Billy said morosely.

"No, he won't," his mother smiled. "I won't let him."

Later, in bed in the loft, Billy heard his parents talking softly below. His father's voice sounded grim, and his mother's gently firm, but there was no anger in either of them. He felt better, hearing this. Maybe everything was going to work out just fine, he told himself. He thought about his hawk up on the mountain with McGraw. It was really going to be a good hawk, he thought. He and Mc-Graw would make it so. Billy imagined flying the hawk, seeing it out in the sky, free, and then hurtling back to his signal. Thinking about this made him momentarily forget everything else that might complicate life in general for him or his family, or even for McGraw, and he felt a keen anticipation, a renewal of his spirit. The way he loved the hawk was just unbelievable. He was going to make it the best hawk in the world, and people would come from all around to watch it fly, hunt, and return perfectly to his glove. You could do anything if you tried hard enough, and he was going to make the hawk perfect.

The prospect was so exciting he could hardly contain it. It was going to be great fun, all of it.

Maybe even enough to compensate for the trouble with Paw—and the feeling that came when he thought about it.

Eight

Training a hawk, McGraw told Billy, was not a thing that dragged out. A hawk would either train, or he wouldn't. You pushed right along on the thing and found out within a month, ordinarily.

"As I see it," McGraw told Billy thoughtfully one evening, while the two of them squatted on the ground, watching the hawk sit on his perch and keep a keen but unfrightened eye on them, "this particular hawk has a lot going for it in terms of being a pet, and a lot going against it in terms of ever being a real hunter."

"He'll be a good pet and a good hunter both," Billy argued, watching his hawk's magnificent eyes pivot to the sound of his voice.

"Maybe so," McGraw grunted. He rubbed one brawny forearm with a work-gnarled hand, sort of fluffing up the thatch of man-hair that was already gray, too old-looking for the deep muscles of the arm. "Problem is, he was the runt of the litter. In nature, he'd be long gone by now. Dead. Gobbled up by a fox, the way you told it."

"I saved him, though," Billy pointed out.

"Right, but that's not natural."

110

"Heck, I'm as natural as the next thing. I'm as natural as a dadgummed ole fox! Just because my hawk had good luck instead of bad luck, that doesn't mean it isn't natural. All natural luck doesn't have to be *bad*."

McGraw smiled, his entire face wrinkling. "I guess you've got a point."

"My hawk will be just fine."

"I hope so. I hope he doesn't become too much a pet."

Billy moved forward, off his haunches, and raised his arm toward the hawk. The hawk flapped its wings enormously and rose off the perch to the end of its jesses, making dirt fly from the ground below and really creating a noisy commotion.

"Does *that* look like he's too much of a pet?" Billy asked.

McGraw sighed and shook his head. "I get the feeling he'd better *not* be too much of a pet, and he'd better not make any other serious mistakes, either. You're about the stubbornest kid with wild creatures that I've ever run into."

"I'm not stubborn with 'em," Billy protested. "I'm nice to 'em. I know what they can do and what they can't. I just try to make 'em do the right thing, as far as you can make any critter do what you want."

"Precisely," McGraw said. "And you'll make a hunter of this hawk if it's the last thing you do, right?"

"Hawks learn. You know how to teach 'em. I can do the work. I don't know why we can't make him a good hawk that's happy with us and all."

"Billy," McGraw said softly, "sometimes things just don't work out, boy. You ought to *remember* that."

"I will," Billy said, ignoring the thought that McGraw was trying to tell him something he deemed most serious. "Now what do we do with our dumb ole hawk today?"

The hawk, having learned to accept small morsels from the stick, had been learning for the last two days to take larger pieces of raw meat tossed in front of his perch. He had to hop to the ground for these, then tear them with his powerful talons and beak before swallowing them. It was, McGraw explained, a big step for the hawk to make, especially since it had to learn this new method of eating while being watched at a discreet distance by a couple of big, ornery critters who were responsible for the jesses, which he still wasn't used to, by any means.

By the end of the week, however, the hawk was not only eagerly eating the meat tossed in front of it on its outside perch, it was accepting the jesses—and the presence of Billy and McGraw—with much more equanimity. Billy, knowing hawks had to have roughage, bones, and feathers to keep their digestion straight, had been catching some small sparrows and offering these to the hawk. It got to the place by the end of the week that the hawk knew whether Billy had a dead sparrow for it before Billy was even halfway up the last rise from the woods to the house. If he had a sparrow, the hawk cried and spread its wings, moving around nervously, in anticipation. If Billy was empty-handed, the hawk just sat there like some regal king, giving him the cold-eyed stare.

"He's getting trained to expect the sparrows," Billy told McGraw, "and that's good."

"I think he figures he's getting you trained to bring them, only sometimes you're a little dumb and forget," McGraw said.

The dead sparrows were the sort of thing that Billy would not tell his mother. She would say it was cruel. As a matter of fact, Billy didn't like catching the sparrows at all, and killing them was even worse. But hawks had some kind of a mechanism in their digestive systems: Once or twice a week, if they'd been fed properly, they brought up a pellet of ball-shaped hair about the size of Billy's thumb,

112

and this ball cleansed them inside. McGraw had cut a pellet open for Billy and showed him the bones and bits of undigestible stuff inside. Without a bird or some mice or similar hairy-feathery prey, hawks could get sick and waste away, McGraw said. So whether Billy was getting trained to bring the sparrows, or the hawk was getting trained to expect them, it really didn't matter. It was good for everybody.

A lot of the early feeding was done in the shed, which was quite dim, or on the outside perch late in the evening when it was nearing darkness. "We increase the light a little at a time," McGraw explained. "This old hawk has to get used to everything gradual." And it was all done a tiny step at a time. But each day another step was added according to a timetable and wisdom of McGraw's that Billy seldom could guess the day before, so progress was steady.

Despite his chores, Billy managed to get up the mountain every day at one time or another, and he soon learned that McGraw, although he was lavishing great attention on the hawk, had plenty of other things to keep him busy, too.

The animals were a part of it. McGraw provided all his own food by hunting with simple snares or by fishing in the cold snow-melt stream a hundred yards below his cliffside dugout. Billy had imagined he himself knew a few things about hunting and fishing, but McGraw made him look like a babe in the woods. Even at that, hunting and fishing were a small part of McGraw's activity. The other animals—the ones he was nursing or raising—were what filled his days.

He had, besides the hawk, five "patients" in what he called his animal hospital. There was the fawn, recovering slowly from what had surely been a near-fatal attack by a lion; the owl, which had tangled with something much too

113

mean for it and lost part of a wing in the process; a wolf cub, whose paw had been terribly mangled in a cruel metal-jawed trap; a fat old bobcat who never did any harm, but just seemed too lazy to hunt for food any more when McGraw would provide it if she slunk in close enough, and gave him a doleful enough look; and of course Bodacious, the mule, McGraw's property by right of the fact that the original owner had planned to shoot it and McGraw had intervened, saying even *that* kind of break might be mended with enough luck and patience.

The fawn had the high-fenced pen for its domain, and the owl always hung around the shed roof or a nearby tree. It had been touch and go with the wolf cub for a while, and it still stayed in a fenced enclosure beside McGraw's own sleeping quarters. The bobcat only appeared in time for food, and then at a haughty distance. Bodacious, being a mule, walked all over the place, knocked down clotheslines and got in the garden quite a lot.

"Get out of there, you old ninny!" McGraw bellowed once when Bodacious was waltzing around through the bush beans. "You old reprobate! Do you want your rear end kicked for you?"

Bodacious raised one ear, yawned, and sauntered through the peas to get to the hole in the smooth-wire fence he had knocked earlier.

Fuming, McGraw patched wire while Billy watched the hawk.

"Why don't you use bob wire?" Billy asked.

"No," McGraw said shortly, twisting strands of smooth stuff together.

"It'd sure keep him outta your garden."

"I don't hold to barbed wire," McGraw told him, leaning on his fence tool for a moment. "For one thing, it's cruel. Have you ever seen a cow or a bull or a deer that caught

114

its leg in barbed wire? I've seen them hobbling on stumps, where they sawed clear through. No, sir. No barbed wire for me. Even if it wasn't cruel, I still wouldn't like it."

"How come?" Billy asked.

"It's cutting this whole country up," McGraw said, his eyes distantly angry.

"The country's gotta be tamed," Billy pointed out.

"Who says so?" McGraw shot back.

"Well, my paw, for one."

McGraw promptly changed his expression and tone. "Well, I'm sure he must be right. I sure wouldn't argue with him. But this used to be a big land, you know that? You could go from the Bravo to Canada and never touch wire. But not now. Not now. It ain't such a big country any more, Billy. By the time you're grown, it won't be big at all; it'll just be a collection of little old farms, and you won't be able to walk a hundred yards without a 'by your leave' or a 'pardon me.'"

"It's gonna be all right for me," Billy told the older man, "because I'm gonna live on a mountain. Like you."

McGraw's weathered face split in a broad grin. "Oh, you are, are you."

"Right. And I'm going to help sick animals, too."

"The rate things are going, there won't be any animals left by then."

"Aw! There'll always be plenty of animals!"

McGraw cupped his hands to his eyes and squinted at the sky. "Not as much ducks and geese as there used to be. Sky used to be black with them. Not now. The buffalo is finished. They'll do the same thing to the passenger pigeon, you mark my words. Ladies like the feathers too much. Then they'll cut down woods, shoot eagles and birds like your hawk, here, and there won't be any natural habitat, no parents to continue the strain, and it'll be all over." Mc-

115

Graw's voice took on a metallic, bitter ring. "Some of the trappers and such ought to be happy then. *Nothing* out here, just them and their traps, waiting in case some baby of something gets born and needs killing off real fast."

Billy took a deep breath. "You don't like folks too much, do you."

McGraw shrugged. "I know them."

"Is that why you live on a mountain? Because you dislike folks so much?"

"I don't dislike 'em, boy. Don't talk foolishness. I *know* them, I said, that's all. Do you cuss the wolf because he hunts a rabbit? Do you blame the hawk for trying to catch a frog or a little snake or a warbler to eat? That's the way nature *is*. It's not good and it's not bad, it just *is*. That's the way it is with people, too. No sense blaming them. Man is the worst hunter because he's smartest, and he likes killing more than any other creature. He's the cruelest, and when he doesn't have anything else to do, he kills off his own kind."

McGraw sighed. "But that's just nature, like I said. Do you want to work some with your hawk?"

Once they started working with the hawk, the scales of cynicism fell away from the older man, and he was like a boy again—chuckling, smiling, exercising infinite patience, watching Billy and gently teasing him sometimes, yet never betraying the slightest sign of cruelty.

It seemed that there was a tremendous amount for the hawk to learn. McGraw took the food chunks, tossed loose on the ground in front of the bird's perch up until now, and tied one or the other of them to a string. When the hawk hopped down to catch the meat, McGraw showed Billy how to tease or jerk the string, giving the hawk some added sport in making tiny midair adjustments. Sometimes the hawk missed and lost its temper and struck the meat

116

a second time, savagely. Getting the hawk to grab food on a line was important, McGraw pointed out, in terms of the next steps, which would come up within a week or two.

While the feeding process was going on, McGraw and Billy also worked on getting the hawk to carry more calmly. At first, with the hawk in its dim shed, on its perch, McGraw moved his gloved arm and fist parallel with the ground, very slowly approaching the hawk's perch position. His forearm pressed the hawk backward, threatening gently to shove him clear off the perch. The hawk flapped his wings wildly and hopped onto McGraw's gloved forearm only long enough to catch balance and hop right back onto the more familiar perch. McGraw had Billy work on the technique after McGraw's arm tired, and it was Billy who finally got the hawk to step up calmly, as if he had been doing it all his life, and perch on Billy's forearm.

"He's doing it!" Billy whispered delightedly. "Look! Hey!"

"Be quiet," McGraw counseled softly. "Just hold real still, now. Let him sit there on your arm a while. See, he's got to do a lot of riding on that arm. Let him get used to it slow. After a while we'll just stand up easy, see if he won't let you carry him around the shed a little—"

But when Billy tried this a few minutes later, the hawk practically went berserk. It flapped its wings frantically and went clear off his arm and jerked on the ends of its jesses and ended up hanging upside down, virtually pulling Billy's arm off and scaring him half out of his wits before McGraw could rush over, grab the hawk by belly and breast, and swing it back to its regular perch.

"I messed it up!" Billy cried disgustedly. "I probably hurt him and everything else! When he started to flap, I got scared. I was stupid!"

McGraw expertly got the jesses looped into the swivels of

117

the perch again, and with his free hand began stroking the hawk with a long feather. As he spoke, his voice crooned to provide the correct tone for gentling the hawk, which trembled and spat fire from its wild eyes.

"You did fine, sonny," he murmured. "The bird's okay, he might have learned a little lesson, even, falling off that way."

"I panicked," Billy said bitterly.

"You're going to make mistakes, Billy. Everybody does. You're doing fine. I'd say we're way ahead of the game, actually, on time. So let's not be feeling bad, okay?"

Billy watched the hawk calming down, and began to feel his own insides settle. He said nothing, however, because he still felt it was all his fault.

"As a matter of fact," McGraw said conversationally, "I'd say you ought to be walking this old bird outside in another three or four days. Might be a good time to bring that friend of yours up with you, about next Monday or Tuesday. You could maybe show him all the hawk's learned, and maybe even walk the hawk around on your arm for his benefit."

Looking at the mountain man, Billy felt a flush of thankfulness and love that almost bowled him over. He had mentioned the possibility of Jeremy visiting, but that had been days ago, and McGraw had shown no sign he even heard the remark. Now McGraw was using this moment to cheer him up and tell him, simultaneously, that it was all right about Jeremy. It was no small thing, letting another person come here, Billy realized now. McGraw wanted his privacy too much—guarded himself from people too carefully to allow casual intruders. He was letting Jeremy come as a favor to Billy, and to let Billy share a moment of triumph with a friend.

"You sure it'll be okay about Jeremy," he said.

118

"No reason why not," McGraw grunted.

"You don't let many people come up."

"Well, *I* know that."

"But it's really all right?"

"Dadblame it, boy! If I didn't think it was all right, I wouldn't *say* it was all right!"

McGraw, Billy was learning, had that facility for being just as tough and cranky as could be. Billy had heard him use language on Bodacious that would have made his mother faint. Yet this same big, slope-shouldered man could turn around from a seeming temper tantrum and be, within seconds, completely calm and exquisitely gentle, soothing a frightened animal or doing some aspect of training with a care and smoothness that seemed almost unreal in its perfect sensitivity. Billy knew that in one way, a way he could not quite understand, he was being handled by McGraw just like the wild things. But he also knew that the older man needed him, somehow, liked him, took pride in him. It was good, the way they worked together sometimes.

"If it's really okay," Billy told McGraw now, "I'll probably bring Jeremy some day real soon."

"Tomorrow is fine."

"Well, not *tomorrow*."

"Why not?"

"I've got some, uh, stuff to do. I might not be able to see him."

McGraw shrugged.

The truth of the matter was that Billy didn't feel quite sure he was ready to bring Jeremy or anyone else up to visit McGraw, or to see the hawk. Faced with the genuine possibility of bringing a friend, he discovered he was not sure he wanted to *share*.

119

Squatting in the dimmed shed, watching his hawk on its perch, he thought out loud about it.

"I ain't selfish," he said softly to the hawk. "Jeremy wants to come up, I know that. And I'll bring him. I'll bring him one day soon. But boy, I don't know if I want to bring him *tomorrow*. I mean, that's *sudden*."

The hawk watched him with fierce, calm eyes.

"You have to get used to other people," Billy told him. "I know that, too. So it's good for ole Jeremy to come. But it just seems like the whole thing is going to be—like it's going to be *public* once he comes, you know?"

The hawk blinked slowly and held its head high, still watching him with the sharpest, keenest attention.

"Maybe that makes me selfish," Billy went on. "Only except for old Alexander the Great, I haven't really ever had something that was *mine*, I mean that I was responsible for, you know? I mean, I like you being mine, and I don't want to share you.

"You're the best-looking hawk anyone ever saw," Billy added feelingly. "I sure don't want you ever to feel bad about not being with your family. I mean, maybe you sit on your perch outside sometimes and see them. Do you? Yeah, I can tell in your expression, you probably do. Well, they're just flying around looking for snakes and dumb stuff like that. You're gonna have a lot better life than them, boy. I mean it. Once you're trained, this trouble with the vigilantes and everything will be over, and you can come live at our house. We'll hunt every day and you'll come when I call you and we'll have a tremendous time, no kidding. You won't feel sorry about not being wild."

The hawk sat perfectly still on its perch, watching him. The eyes were cold—cold and hard and disciplined, yet with some inner glow of a gentler intelligence.

"And you'll like Jeremy real well," Billy added. "He's a nice feller."

The hawk spread some of its feathers, readjusted its weight on the perch, and resumed watching him with an expression of regal fascination.

"See you tomorrow," Billy told him, and left the shed, carefully closing the door behind him.

McGraw came over from the pen, limping slightly. "Heading out now, I suppose, young feller?"

"If I'm gonna get back by dark, I am," Billy replied.

"I'd say everybody ought to be home or out of sight by dark, from what I keep observing of the vigilance committee."

Billy nodded. "They haven't done nothing for a few nights now, but they sure must have burned out the Logans."

"Yes, sir, I'd say so," McGraw agreed darkly. "And they're out these nights, even if nothing is being done—" He shook his head. "They're out."

They walked toward the edge of McGraw's clearing, toward the point where the clearing sloped into brush and began to fall away toward the distant valley floor, already lavender in the evening twilight.

"From what I hear," Billy told McGraw, "things is quieter in town."

"Don't doubt it," McGraw murmured.

"I hear a lot of rough guys up and left."

"I imagine."

"My paw is *right*, I know that," Billy pointed out thoughtfully. "But it sure does look like Mister Carson and his vigilance committee has done some good at that."

"Might be," McGraw grunted. "But I'd still side with your daddy."

"Gosh, he's been real busy, riding around where Sheriff

Sweeney tells him, and stuff, but he hasn't *done* anything."

"You don't talk about your daddy that way," McGraw said sharply.

"I didn't mean any disrespect." Billy was slightly flustered. "All I meant was, what's gotten done, the vigilance guys have done it. Ole Sheriff Sweeney and my paw haven't."

"No. All *they've* done is try to uphold the law." McGraw's tone was whip sharp.

"What're you mad about?" Billy asked. He was upset and hurt.

"Aw," McGraw muttered disgustedly, tossing a heavy arm over his shoulder, "I suppose I just don't like the idea of them smart-alecks taking the law in their own hands and getting kids like you to thinking it's all right. You just don't criticize your daddy, boy. Not really, and not even by saying stuff indirectly. Right? Because your daddy has needed a lot of courage to do what he's been doing, going against his neighbors and all. One day you'll understand that."

"Okay," Billy said shamefacedly. "I'll keep my big trap shut."

"Maybe you ought to have some cookies to put in that trap on the walk back home," McGraw added, obviously wanting to make him feel better.

"I better not," Billy said. "If I don't eat all my supper, my mom threatens to take my hide off."

McGraw chuckled through his nose the way he did when he was really tickled. "See you tomorrow. And bring your buddy!"

Billy hurried down the mountainside and cut cross-country, going for his home place as fast as he could jog. It was going to be touch and go, whether he made it before dark. He had cut it awfully close several nights, and had

122

gotten good and bawled out for it. He knew his parents' anger was in direct proportion to their worry about him when he was off someplace for hours on end, and even though they knew now that he was going up the mountain on most of the trips, they worried just as much as if he were off for parts unknown.

Running along a hill saddle and down through a meadow, Billy made his plans to notify Jeremy that it was okay to come along with him, and then he got busy imagining what he would show Jeremy about the hawk, how the hawk would act, how impressed Jeremy would be, what would be said, how Jeremy and McGraw would get along, and how it would be good to have company on these hurried long hikes home in the late evenings. Jeremy might not be able to run with him all this way, Billy thought; Jeremy was messing around with cigarettes fairly regularly now, and your wind went when you did that. But it would be good to have company anyhow.

The way things looked—despite McGraw's warnings—the trouble in the valley was definitely easing off, too. As far as Billy knew, nobody had been killed. Certainly there had been no lynchings. The last couple of days had seemed really quiet, and even his father had evidently begun to worry less about the situation that had forced him to become a most unlikely deputy. With that stuff easing, and his hawk coming right along, and McGraw for a new friend, Billy felt it could turn out to be the best summer by far that he had ever known. The positive feelings were so strong that he got a second wind, jogging through the meadow toward the creek line and trees, and he ran harder and faster.

He was running just about full out, as a matter of fact, when a rope or branch or something hit him across the chest and knocked him sprawling.

123

Nine

Billy had just cut into the creek line, with its fringe of cottonwoods and junipers, when the heavy blow took him across the chest and jerked him backward off his feet. He hit the dirt hard, shocked out of thought. Spitting dirt, he rolled over and saw that a looped rope had jerked tight across his chest, causing his fall. He sat up and pulled the tight loop to free himself.

"Just leave it there and don't move."

The voice was close, in the trees, and familiar. Before he located its source he knew the speaker was Morrie Carson.

Carson it was, all right—coming out of hiding and looping his lariat back into shape as he approached Billy. There were some horses back in the trees, and Billy saw them before he realized that Morrie was not alone; there were three other boys in the tree shade with him. Billy recognized Cruble, Zengler, and Robertson. It had been Robertson with Morrie that other time, but Billy had no time to speculate upon this, or his surprise that the other two were with them, at the moment.

His Levi's and blue jacket dusty from a ride, Morrie

124

Carson paused about six feet from where Billy sprawled in the dirt and grinned down at him, keeping the rope taut. "You're in an awful hurry, Billy boy."

"What do you want?" Billy demanded. "Git that rope *off* me!"

"In a minute, in a minute," Morrie crooned. "Just as soon as you answer a few questions."

"I don't have to answer any questions for you guys!"

Robertson stepped forward and nudged him with the toe of his boot. "Where you been and what've you been doing?"

Billy hesitated. All four of them were a head or more taller than he, and two or more years older. He was surprised to see Cruble and Zengler, as a matter of fact, because he had figured they were through with school, working full-time, and in the world of men. Now here they were with Morrie and Robertson. What was going on?

He decided to play it as cautiously as he could. "I've been out on some errands."

"Errands?" Morrie asked.

"Looking for berries," Billy lied.

"*This* time of year?"

"Well, I'm too early, but I thought I'd check."

"That's pretty stupid of you, Billy boy," Morrie said.

"A family can use all the food it can get," Billy shot back, "when somebody like your paw cuts off credit at the store."

"Don't talk against my father, buddy, unless you want—"

"Take it easy, take it easy," Robertson cut in nervously. "All we're trying to do is collect information, remember?"

Flushed with anger, Morrie nodded and took the rope over Billy's head. "This is the second time we've seen you come down this way in the past few days. Where have you really been? Up to see the crazy man?"

"He isn't crazy," Billy said without thinking. Then he

125

added quickly, "No. I wouldn't go see any crazy man. I—"

"What's going on with you and the crazy man?" Morrie demanded. "What kind of business? Does your father know?"

"What business is it of *yours?*" Billy fired back. "Who do you think you are? What are you doing out here like this, anyway?"

"Everybody does his share," Morrie said grimly. "We're collecting information."

"Why? For who? *I* haven't done anything!"

"The vigilance committee wants to know everything," Morrie said. "If a person collects information that leads to an arrest or an action by the committee, there's a ten-dollar reward."

"What are you going to do?" Billy asked sarcastically. "Collect for saying I like to walk in the woods?"

Morrie balled a fist and stepped forward. "You little punk, I ought to—"

"Take it easy, Morrie!" Robertson pleaded.

"Yeah, Morrie," Zengler whined. "Let's ride on out of here and see if we can find anything someplace else."

"Right," Cruble said. "I agree with that. Leave this kid alone."

Morrie hesitated. He would have liked to trouble Billy further; it was obvious. But he had his buddies to cope with.

He walked around Billy, kicking dirt insolently. "You'd better be more careful. If you're smart, you'll stay away from the crazy man."

"Is that so?" Billy breathed, a new kind of worry striking into him.

"It's not smart to arouse suspicion right now," Morrie told him.

For an instant Billy had had the feeling that it was a

126

direct threat against both him and McGraw. Now he felt that he had been wrong, that Morrie's words had been general bluster. Despite the situation of the moment, he relaxed slightly inside.

"Thanks for the advice." He forced himself to be just about 100 percent more polite than he felt.

"Just remember it," Morrie said.

Billy stood there and watched them walk into the trees to their horses. They swung into the saddles, turned, and rode away, headed in the general direction of town.

Limping a little where he had skinned and bruised his leg, Billy picked up his pace and resumed jogging through the tree line, headed for the fields on the far side that led toward his home.

It was so dadblamed stupid, he thought, the four of them almost grown men, riding around, playing vigilante. It was just ridiculous. But this did not change the fact that they were a lot bigger than he, that Morrie had a genuine cruel streak in him, and that they could cause him more trouble than he wanted if they set their minds to it. They were dummies, sure. But he had to start taking them into consideration from here on out if he planned to continue visiting McGraw and working with his hawk. They were not above really messing him up if he wasn't careful.

He hurried on home. Some stars were clear in the gray-blue sky as he trotted down the road. Rex, hearing or seeing him coming a half-mile away, started barking like mad, and a flock of sparrows took out of the wood behind the garden and scattered over the sky. Good food for the hawk there, if a man had a big enough net. . . .

"Aw, shut up, you big dummy!" he yelled as Rex came loping out onto the road, still barking at him. Rex, recognizing his voice, instantly went all to pieces, wagging so fast and hard that his hind end threatened to fly around

127

in front, and coming down the road to greet him with ears up and tongue lollygagging halfway to the ground.

They met in the roadway, Rex licked him a big, wet, smeary good one, he yelled *"Yuk!"* at the top of his lungs, and they raced the rest of the way to the house. Rex won, naturally, and was sitting on the porch, wagging all over again, when Billy got there.

"Just keep that dog out!" his mother called sharply as he started in.

"I am!" he called.

His mother was at the fireplace, swinging a kettle of beans and pork off the wood flames. Smoke made the room gray at the edges, but it smelled good and the mountain evening had turned just cool enough for the smoke and fire to feel good, too.

"You're late," she said sternly.

"Yes, ma'am." He knew better than to argue.

She sighed and frowned at him with her hands on her hips. "Well," she said finally, "hurry and wash up."

"Where's Paw?" he asked, pumping up water at the sink.

"He had to go to town. He should be back soon."

"Is there trouble?"

"Not that I know of," she said in a tone that made it clear she was not at all sure.

Billy mopped his face and arms, and dried off.

"Do behind your ears!"

"Yes, ma'am."

"I'm going to go ahead and feed you because I don't know exactly when your father will get in."

"Yes, ma'am."

"The cornbread will be finished in just a minute, so go ahead and sit down."

"How come we have beans and cornbread?" Billy asked,

128

taking his place at the table. "I thought we were out of beans and cornmeal *both*."

"Well," Mom said, getting that haughty look she got when her pride was really near the surface, "our credit at the store was made good again. So we did some shopping."

"Why'd they give us back our credit?" He was astonished.

Mom put the plate of steaming food in front of him. "Mister Carson said he didn't want to make it seem like the store was retaliating against people. He said he knew everyone has to follow his own conscience. He isn't a bad man, son. He and most of the people around here are really very nice."

"Oh, yeah," Billy grunted. "Just as long as you do what they want."

"That's not true, and it's a terrible thing to say! If it *were* true, we wouldn't have our credit back."

"We would if what we did on the vigilante deal didn't make any difference one way or the other to them."

"I'm not at all sure I approve of this cynical attitude, young man."

He decided to be smart and say absolutely nothing at all.

She placed a round pan of golden cornbread on the table at his side. The aroma was sweet and overpowering, and while she cut slices, he gouged big chunks of fresh butter out of the deep dish and piled them on the first couple of pieces of bread out of the pan. It seemed really strange to be home like this, having a feast, just a little while after being scared to death by Morrie Carson and his stupid buddies in the creek gully. Things changed very fast sometimes, Billy reflected.

"I suppose you've been off with that strange man and your hawk?" his mother said.

"Yessum." The cornbread, soaked clear through with

fresh-made butter so it dripped out the bottom, was *fantastic.*

"Is the hawk going to live?"

"Oh, sure! It's fine! We're training it now."

"Training it? How?"

"Well, teaching it to ride on the glove, stuff like that."

"Son—what will you do—after it's all trained?"

"Do?" He didn't quite understand.

Her expression showed strain. "Will you bring it home then?"

"Well, I didn't think so. Paw said he didn't want any more critters."

"Will you leave it with the cra—with your friend up there?"

"Mister McGraw would keep it if I asked him," Billy said with a sense of outraged dignity. *"Mister* McGraw is real good with animals. *Mister* McGraw is a real nice man: kind, gentle, smart, and he minds his own business and doesn't spend half his time gouging folks in a store, like *some* folks we have to mess with around this town."

"Billy," she said, coming out with it, evidently, "are you *sure* your Mister McGraw is all right? I mean, really *all right?"*

"He ain't crazy."

"I didn't mean that! People—talk, Billy. I've heard it said that no one knows where this man comes from, or why he insists on living alone the way he does. Does he always act all right to you? Is there a chance he might—have something bad in his past? Be a criminal?"

"He lives alone because he likes it," Billy said angrily. "His past is his own dadblamed business, *I'd* say. And heck no, he always acts fine when I'm around! I don't think you need to worry at all, Mom! I mean it."

130

She sighed. "I do, though. All mother's worry. Now, with the investigation—" She stopped suddenly.

Billy chilled. "The what?"

"Nothing, dear. Eat your food before it gets—"

"Is somebody investigating Mister McGraw?"

"Well, not just him, certainly, and there's nothing to be concerned about—"

"Mom, *tell* me!"

She frowned. "Dear, there just isn't that much to tell. Your father said the vigilance committee has started investigating quite a list of people in and around Springer. There are supposed to be more than two dozen names on the list. They—"

"What are they doing? How are they doing it?"

"In most cases, writing letters, finding where people came from, talking to their neighbors—"

"Yeah! Snooping!"

"Your father doesn't like it any better than you do, son. But the vigilance people are doing it; they say they're determined to find out if any undesirable element is in the area."

"Mister Carson will think Mister McGraw is pretty undesirable," Billy said bitterly. "Mister McGraw doesn't buy many groceries from him!"

"I want you to be calm about this, Billy. It does no good to lose your temper. Whatever happens, you just be sure you be polite, and tell the truth."

"What do you mean, 'whatever happens'?" he demanded, thoroughly alarmed now. He was beginning to realize that he still didn't know why Paw was in town, or why she was making such an issue of Mister McGraw, and he had an idea about it, a sudden one, which he didn't like.

"They heard I've been visiting up there, is that it?" he

asked. He read her expression and remembered Morrie Carson simultaneously. Both confirmed his suspicion. "What do they want to do? Ask me questions about him? Ask me to *spy* on him for 'em?"

"That's why your father is in town, son. He won't let them question you or bother you. You should know that. You don't have to worry about it."

He stared at his mother, thunderstruck by the knowledge that it had already come to this. His father would keep them from bothering him, he thought. Especially since he was a sort of a deputy, he had the authority to keep them from coming around and snooping here.

But that didn't mean they would leave McGraw alone in other ways. If he was on a list somewhere, he would be checked. There were grown men in Springer with the instincts of Morrie Carson, merely more developed and honed. They were learning, perhaps, to like to check up on other people, and run off "undesirables."

McGraw, Billy saw, was on the brink of serious trouble.

Jeremy's eyes shone with controlled excitement as Billy proudly made the introductions. "How do you do, sir," Jeremy said.

McGraw shook hands courteously. "I'm pleased you could visit, young man. Jeremy, is it? Fine name. Biblical. Billy tells me you like animals the same as he and I do."

"Yessir," Jeremy said eagerly, his Adam's apple going up and down. "But I don't have a bunch like Billy does."

"I suppose you'd like to see young Mister Baker's hawk, too, eh?"

"Well, sir—"

"Tell you what," McGraw said with a smile. "I've got a pretty fawn in that pen over there, and if you move slowly, you'll get a close-up look at the ugliest owl you ever saw in

132

your life. He sits on the side of the chimney and pretends he's invisible. Meanwhile, I'll give your partner, here, a hand in bringing out the hawk."

"Yessir," Jeremy nodded, pleased.

"Come on, falcon master," McGraw said, putting an arm over Billy's shoulder.

They walked to the shed, where Billy opened the outer door carefully and slowly, as he had been taught, to make sure the hawk did not panic at the change in light. He and McGraw went inside. As usual, the shed smelled strongly of the hawk's excrement. The hawk sat calmly enough on its floor-mounted perch, watching them.

"Hello, you ole dummy," Billy said. He could have sworn the hawk showed recognition.

"I guess the best thing to do," McGraw said softly, "is for you to carry him out and put him on the perch. That way your friend Jeremy can get a good look. Then we can go ahead with some food training."

"Fine," Billy muttered, getting tense, as he always did when he was to handle the hawk.

McGraw handed him the glove and armguard. "Make sure to transfer the jesses and keep a good grip on them with your thumb."

Billy nodded and took the glove and waited.

McGraw stood there watching him. An awkward moment passed.

"Well?" McGraw said finally, a trace of a smile on his lips.

"I'm waiting for you to hood him," Billy said.

"Let's try it without the hood this time."

Billy blinked and couldn't move for a moment. "It's *bright* out there!" he protested. As a matter of fact, it was far brighter than it had been at any time when he had

133

carried the hawk on his arm without the hood as a calming device. Now McGraw, in suggesting that they carry the hawk out of the relatively dim shed into the sudden bright light of late afternoon, was pressing him into a doubly new and scary trial for both him and the hawk: both brighter light and sharper transition into the brightness. "This ole hawk might go looney when I carry him out there!"

"Well now," McGraw said softly, "he might at that. But I don't think so—not unless you go looney first, and show how nervous *you* are. This hawk is smarter than you give him credit for sometimes. He's learning real fast. He knows you. He acts different when you're in here, compared with the way he acts when I'm here by myself. He likes you."

Billy didn't want to try it. The idea was too new. "As *big* as he's gotten, I don't even know if I can carry him that far! I mean, he's gotten to be a big ole hawk!"

"If you don't want to try it, Billy, then don't." McGraw was watching him closely, compassion and a lively amusement in his crinkled eyes. "A man should never do something he really doesn't want to do."

"I *want* to," Billy breathed. "I'd *sure* like to carry this hawk out there and have Jeremy see me do it. But I just don't know if I can do it right."

"You can do it right."

"And I don't know if the ole hawk—"

"He's ready, Billy. You both are—if you think you are."

Billy looked from McGraw's lined, solemn face to the hawk, and back again. He struggled with himself. He trusted McGraw. McGraw just would not be wrong about something like this.

"Whatever you think," McGraw told him softly. "If you feel like you want to give this hawk another few days, that's real fine. It won't hurt to wait a few days."

134

McGraw, Billy realized, was giving him an easy out. That somehow helped him decide.

"I'll do it," he said quickly.

"Okay, mighty fine," McGraw said as if he had known it all along.

Billy put the glove and gauntlet on his right arm, then walked very slowly up to the hawk on its perch. The hawk pivoted his head to watch him, unblinking.

Sweat stinging his eyes, Billy knelt and unsnapped the jesses from their perch swivels. This left over a foot of twin leather lines attached to the hawk's legs, and these he twisted around his thumb and pinched inside his palm to make absolutely sure that the bird would not get away if it panicked and tried to fly.

The hawk watched this operation with interest, but made no move.

Billy held his arm out in front of the hawk's chest and legs, and moved it toward the legs, planning to nudge them gently. It wasn't even necessary. The hawk stepped up onto his gloved arm with perfect ease and calm.

"Did you see that?" Billy said, thrilled.

"Now just carry him right out," McGraw said softly. "I told you there wouldn't be any trouble. Go nice and slow, and don't look right into his eyes, remember. If he starts to flap his wings, you just stand still and keep your face turned. I don't think he'll do that, but he could, if he lost his balance or grip."

"What do I do if he *does* get all wild? Besides stand still and keep my face turned, I mean?"

"I'll help you. Don't worry."

Billy took a gentle breath and rose slowly to his feet with his hawk on his arm. He walked toward the door. It was *so* much brighter!

"Okay," McGraw said gently.

Billy walked outside, flinching as the sun struck him and the bird on his arm.

The hawk did not budge.

Near the fenced pen, Jeremy turned and looked awed, his mouth fallen open. "Gosh!" he said huskily.

"Nice and quiet, boy," McGraw told Jeremy. "And just stay right there."

Jeremy stood his ground. Billy, holding his breath, walked across the yard. He was so proud he felt like he was going to just blow up and go all over the sky in pieces. The hawk looked around with interest, but rode on his arm as if they had been doing it for years. *This* was what having a hawk was all about, he thought with a thrill. He and the hawk understood each other. In the weight and the slight, living tension of talons on heavy leather glove, there was a communication. He didn't have to look at his hawk. The hawk did not have to be able to speak or even signal. They knew each other. They were partners right in this very instant, and they both understood it.

Billy walked to the yard perch, knelt, and carefully moved the hawk toward it. The hawk inspected the perch. Billy held his arm still in front of it and didn't rush things. The hawk thought about it and then stepped off his arm and onto the perch.

Billy untangled the jesses and snapped them onto the new perch swivels.

"Good work, boy!" McGraw said proudly, clapping him on the back as he got shakily to his feet and removed the leather glove.

"Gosh, Billy!" Jeremy gasped, coming a step closer. "That was—that's a real beautiful hawk, and you really know how to handle him, don't you!"

Billy's knees, if they had been any more watery, would have pooled out onto the ground.

136

McGraw, of course, acted pretty much like nothing at all unusual had taken place. After his first exclamation of pleasure, he had made it a point to shove his hands into his pockets and stand there as lackadaisically as possible.

"Good thing the bird's in such a good mood today," he said now.

Billy started to ask, but Jeremy asked for him, all awe, "Why's that, sir?"

McGraw's lips quirked in a smile. "He's got a couple new lessons coming this afternoon."

"What're they?" Jeremy asked, excited.

Jeremy looked to Billy for an answer, of course, and Billy did his best to freeze his face and hide the fact that he didn't have any idea what the new lessons were going to be. It made him realize how dependent he was upon McGraw for teaching the hawk; if McGraw were to abandon him right now, he would be in bad shape trying to figure out how to proceed with making the hawk into a trained hunter.

Before Billy had to admit his ignorance, McGraw said quietly, "Billy figures the hawk needs exercise, first of all. It's sure time the bird started getting more of that again, right, Billy?"

"Uh, right."

"Then, of course, we have to feed him as usual. But we keep adding new little deals to the feeding, to make it part of the training process."

"Can I watch it all?" Jeremy asked. "I won't scare him by being here or nothing?"

"I think it'll be fine," McGraw told him.

The question of exercise began to be clarified before Billy could form questions about it. McGraw limped to a small lean-to beside the entrance to his cave-house and brought out some coiled lines and swivels and things. Billy saw

137

Jeremy looking everything over with great impression, gawking up the face of the yellow-tan cliff, too, and at the way McGraw had boarded over part of the big old cave to make it into a natural house. The cliff, the cave, the pens and sheds and animals were all familiar to Billy by now, and he scarcely noticed them. He was busy watching McGraw come back with the lines and fasteners; he was trying to figure out what McGraw had on his mind.

It quickly became apparent. McGraw squatted in front of the hawk and fitted swivels from a vee tied to the end of the long, coiled line to the jess swivels holding the hawk to the ground perch. This in effect gave the hawk as much potential freedom as the length of the coiled cord, and it looked like as much as fifty yards—tough, woven twine that had a glint to it as if a very fine wire or two were woven in for added strength.

With the new swivels attached, McGraw signaled to Billy to put the glove back on again and pick the hawk up once more. Billy did so carefully, but the hawk was still in a good mood and hopped right up onto his arms. McGraw carried the coiled twine and led the way downslope from the house and outbuildings, across the sloping shale surface made barren by rain and wind and the erosion of the centuries off the cliff. He looked around thoughtfully, measuring things with his eyes, and then stopped and planted his feet firmly in a spot that placed him just about equidistant from the cliff behind him, the buildings to his left, lower-level rock outcroppings off to the right, and the beginnings of the woods ahead of him and below.

He dropped the coiled line onto the ground and gently lifted loops, making sure it was all untangled. Billy stood a few feet from him with the hawk heavy on his forearm, and Jeremy stood back a dozen respectful paces nearer the outbuildings.

138

"What we do," McGraw said loudly enough for Jeremy to hear, "is fly the hawk on the line. He gets exercise and he gets the idea that he can't just fly off and leave us when we let him go. I hold the end of the line, here, to make sure he doesn't make off with our string. Billy, you fly him."

McGraw held his bare arm out parallel with the ground and bent at the elbow, as it was when holding the hawk. Demonstrating, he lowered the arm platform slightly, then made a quick raising motion.

"You give him this little warning by lowering the arm, see, and then you toss him."

"He's never really flown before," Billy said nervously. "I don't know if he's ready."

McGraw's teeth shone. "If he's not, he'd better *get* ready."

"What if he can't fly?"

"He can fly."

Billy swallowed the lump in his throat. McGraw had always been right. He had to be accepted this time, too.

"Tell you what, Jeremy," McGraw called. "You might want to stand back there in the shade of the buildings. No telling which direction this fool bird will want to go, and the cord won't let him get quite that far."

Jeremy loped for the shed. "I'll stand real still, so's to not spook him any."

"Good," McGraw said. "It's nice to work with people who understand nature and animals."

Jeremy, grinning with obvious flushed pride, leaned against the shed.

McGraw looked back to Billy. "All right, boy. Any time." He held the end of the line.

Billy looked at the hawk. The hawk seemed to have no idea that he was now attached to a very long cord rather than the few inches that usually held him to the perch or the arm. He was big, the hawk was now, and maybe even a little fat, thanks to all the good food. He looked just a little sleepy, his eyes partially closed yet still vigilant.

Billy mightily hated to toss the hawk because he didn't know if he could do it right and he didn't know what the hawk would do and he was afraid it was going to be a real mess.

"You can do it," McGraw said gently.

Billy took a breath and lowered his arm slightly. The hawk widened his eyes and got slightly unsettled, fluttering one wing a bit. His talons gripped tighter to Billy's arm through the leather. Billy lowered his arm a little more, thinking, *If you've got to fly, the higher I throw you the better your chances are.*

He threw his arm upward so hard that he left the ground momentarily with both feet.

The hawk went into the air, straight up, and his big wings unfolded fully for the first time Billy had seen them. The wings made an incredible commotion and the hawk started to drop and then it caught itself and started out across the clearing, heading for the tree line below, rising slightly as it flew hard and steadily, its wings rhythmic.

It was so lovely that it made Billy's throat ache, the way the hawk climbed in this moment's flight, its head forward, leaner and wilder in flight than at rest, headed for the trees.

Beside Billy, McGraw raised the end of the line and made a quick pumping action, sending a high wave action out along the cord. It caught the hawk just as the bird was nearing the end of the line and Billy was seeing for the first time that the shock of reaching the end of the line might be very bad. The wave action shortened the line, and the hawk felt the tug as it reached the end, but then the wave straightened out so that the hawk had some leeway before actually reaching the end of the cord. The warning broke the hawk's flight and it fluttered to the ground and sat still.

140

"*Gee!*" Billy gasped. "Did you *see* him?"

"Go get him," McGraw said with a smile, "and we'll let him do it again."

"Did you see how he *flew*, though? I mean, he's *strong!* And fast—he was starting to pick up speed, and getting some altitude! If it hadn't been for the line, he would have just taken on off and gone over the mountain!"

McGraw chuckled. "I noticed."

Their eyes met and Billy burst out, "Aw, he's so *beautiful!*"

"You want to go get him, sonny, so he can fly again, or do you figure on letting him sit out there all night?"

Billy ran partway down the slope with the exuberance he felt, but then he remembered to slow down and approach the hawk cautiously. If he was worried about the hawk getting too excited in this new situation, again he had underestimated the hawk. The bird watched him calmly and stepped right up onto the glove when it was offered.

Billy carried him back to the center of the sloped clearing, made sure McGraw was ready, and tossed again. This time the hawk took off for the rock formation to the right, and again he landed awkwardly but gently enough at the end of the line. Billy ran and retrieved him again.

"Looks like he'd try to circle," he said, breathing hard from running.

"He'll learn," McGraw promised. "Most hawks, though, start out this way. They fly to the end of the line, straight, and stop."

On his third flight, the hawk headed toward the cliff. On the fourth, he went for the woods again. On the fifth, he started for the sheds, but didn't fly quite as hard or fast, and remained nearer the ground, skimming the rock surface. He landed before he reached the end of the line.

"What's wrong with him?" Billy asked.

141

McGraw guffawed. "He's fat and lazy, that's what's wrong!"

Billy didn't appreciate McGraw laughing or making that kind of comment, but he said nothing as he ran to retrieve the hawk again. He brought it back and tossed it again, and it flew only about halfway out to the end of its line and landed slowly on the downslope toward the woods.

"Fat and lazy," McGraw repeated, chuckling again. "I guess he's had enough for one day."

Putting the hawk back on its regular outdoor perch, Billy decided that getting tired after a half-dozen flights was no big disgrace for a hawk that had really never flown at all before. He figured McGraw was trying to get his goat, talking about the bird being fat and lazy, so he said nothing about that part.

One thing was sure: If the hawk *was* fat and lazy, he would get leaned out now because Billy intended to fly him plenty. This was going to be one world-champion-conditioned hawk before he got through!

With the flying done for the day, however, McGraw wasn't yet finished with new tricks and techniques. When he brought the food out to feed the hawk, it was not done in the usual way. He had Billy toss one piece onto the ground in front of the hawk, and the weary bird was plenty hungry enough to leap upon the mock prey eagerly and tear it with its talons and beak. While the hawk ate this chunk, however, McGraw fastened another piece of meat to an odd contraption Billy had never seen before.

It was a chunk of leather, balled together and tied with thongs and covered with feathers taken off small birds. It had a swiveled connector that allowed McGraw to put a length of twine to it, and it had two short lengths of leather that let him tie the hawk's second piece of meat to its side.

142

With the hawk back on the perch, McGraw tossed the leather object and attached meat onto the ground.

The hawk came down off the perch for it.

McGraw jerked the string briefly, three times, making the hawk grab repeatedly before catching the baited gadget.

Watching the hawk tear the meat off the leather object, McGraw explained to Jeremy, for Billy's benefit: "It all goes a step at a time, youngster. We taught it to eat strips, then we taught it to jump on chunks and tear them up. Now we're teaching it that its food comes looking a lot like natural prey, and that when we show it this lure—that's what the leather deal is called—then it has to grab it to be rewarded. A little later, see, we'll be swinging the lure in the air, and having the hawk catch it in flight. When we get *that* far, we're almost all the way."

McGraw paused, rummaged into his pockets, and brought out a small, slender, wooden object. He handed it to Billy. Billy examined it and saw that it was a whistle, delicately carved out of pine.

"Try it," McGraw suggested.

Billy raised the tube to his lips and blew. A high, piercing whistle sliced the early evening air. The hawk looked up sharply from its feast on the ground.

"You'll call him with the whistle, eventually," McGraw explained. "Course that's a ways off yet. But we'll get there."

Jeremy, who had been watching with eyes that grew wider and wider, finally broke through. "I never *heard* this kind of stuff! Golly, if a hawk can be trained that good in a short time, maybe I could—if I started looking around and located me a nest—"

"No reason why not," McGraw said. He looked at the hawk. "But I'll tell you what. I think *this* old bird has had about all the work he wants for one day."

"Should we put him back inside?" Billy asked.

"No, no reason to. We can let him enjoy the air a while. I've made some cookies you fellers might like. I'd like you to help me with one little job of work, and then we can have us some cookies, if you like."

"It sounds good to me," Billy admitted. "What's the job?"

"Need to walk the fawn down the hill a ways," McGraw said just as if it were nothing, "and turn 'er loose."

"Turn her *loose!*"

"Yep. It's time."

"But you've raised that little thing, Mister McGraw! It's—heck, it's *yours!* I mean, if you hadn't helped it, it'd be dead! Now you going to turn it loose? Don't you *want* it any more?"

"I want it," McGraw said gruffly. "I'm a jelly heart inside. You know that, young feller. But it's time this critter was turned loose. It's past time, most likely—but not too late yet."

Looking at the older man, Billy wanted to ask why— wanted to protest. But the sober expression in McGraw's eyes precluded that. Even Jeremy, new to the entire setting, seemed to recognize that this was no ordinary moment; he watched with big, solemn eyes, his raw-looking hands lax at his sides.

"Not much to the job," McGraw said cheerfully enough, leading them to the large pen beside the sheds. "She's mighty tame, and all I want you boys to do is walk along her flanks, just in case she decides to try to run off in a direction that might get her hurt before she gets her balance."

They reached the pen, and McGraw went inside. The chocolate-colored fawn watched him trustingly, with no sign of alarm, and allowed him to walk up to her, stroke her neck and sides, talk gently to her. Then McGraw slid an arm around the animal's neck and tenderly led it toward the opening in the fence. Billy, seeing what had to be done,

144

slipped around to one side, signaling Jeremy to go to the other. As McGraw moved the fawn slowly through the gate, Billy and Jeremy were on either side, ready to take action if the animal panicked or tried to run into the rocks.

McGraw spoke crooningly to the animal, more to calm it than anything, but the words carried content. "Got to try it on your own again, lady," he said softly. "Yessum, you sure do. You sure do. Wild thing can't stay around a place like this too long, you know. You'd get so tame you'd be no good at all in the wild, and then you'd be beholden to me the rest of your life. You sure would, yessum, you surely would. And what would happen if something was to happen to me, in that case? Why, you'd just be helpless, lady. You'd just die. That's no good, right?"

They moved slowly past the shed and down the slope behind it, with tumbled rocks lining the way on one side and McGraw shielding the other, so the fawn would not bolt down the treacherous shale incline. They moved away from the shade of the towering cliff, away from the house, into the hot, thin sunshine and toward the trees below.

"A wild thing has got to be wild, my lady," McGraw crooned, walking. "Keep you much longer, you'd be a sitting duck for the first lion or wolf you ever came across. Nope, my girl, you have to be turned back to the wild now, while you can still learn. You're strong, and I'll miss you. Sure I will. Sure I will. But it's best."

Still walking the fawn, the three of them awkwardly hemming the docile creature in closely and moving it along toward the trees, they crossed most of the distance from the enclosure to freedom.

McGraw was still talking, but Billy realized that part of it, now, was for him: "Not a lot of wild animals can stay their lives with a man, my lady. No, they can't, they sure can't. A deer can't be like a hawk with a man. A deer

145

grows, she gets fat and lazy and no-account, she gets diseases, dies awfully early. It's better for her to be in the wild. She doesn't have a chance to have a working deal with a man, the way a hawk can."

They reached the first fringe of woods, some waist-high brush and ten-foot saplings just beyond, and here the ground tumbled downward gently into genuine woods only a dozen paces away, dark and deep.

"Step back now, boys," McGraw said softly.

Billy and Jeremy obeyed.

McGraw hugged the fawn's neck. "Go on now, old girl."

The fawn stood there, quiet, watching him. She looked into the woods, but turned back to look at McGraw. She did not want to go.

"Go on, old babe," McGraw said.

Still the animal stood quiet, lovely and sleek and brown.

McGraw quickly slapped her flank, hard.

She bolted, throwing little rocks from her hooves. Two side-stepping leaps, a zigzag motion that was pure grace, and she was into the woods. A tiny branch swayed silently behind her, there was a fleeing shadow, and she was—gone.

Billy felt empty inside, weakened, like something had really gone out of him. He stared at the dark, gentle woods, knowing the fawn might be standing there nearby, watching, invisible—or might be running with silent, gliding freedom a mile away by now. He felt—bereft, and he had been planning to break the subject of the town's questions to McGraw today; he had been thinking, earlier, before all the excitement with the hawk, that he would ask the older man about his past, and warn him that the vigilantes were checking up on him along with certain unknown others.

McGraw still had to be told, Billy thought, but he knew he was not going to broach the subject today. Not now. Not after the fawn.

146

"What do you say we get those cookies now, eh, fellers?" McGraw asked heartily. He patted his belly. "I can use a snack, can't you?"

There were tears in his eyes behind his smile.

Ten

Sheriff Ad Sweeney had spent more than a week straight in Springer, but on the day after Billy first flew his hawk, Sweeney was at the house before dawn, saying he had to ride to the county seat.

"I hope to be back before nightfall," he told Billy's father, while Billy listened from the loft. "I'd appreciate it if you'd go into town and make your presence known."

"Do you expect anything?" Dan Baker asked.

Sweeney paused in the cool black morning. It was very still. Then he said, "No, I don't expect a thing. But you being there—them seeing you—might reduce the chances. There's still a few rowdies around town, and some of our brave citizens are still awful excited about running them out. I don't think you'll have to do anything but *be* there. They know you. This badge still has some weight, too." On the last statement, the sheriff's flat voice became tinged with bitterness.

"I'll go into town in just a little while, then," Dan Baker said.

"I'll appreciate it."

"Have a good ride today."

148

"A hot one, anyway."

"Take care."

"*Adios.*"

When his father came back into the house, trying to be quiet, a stirring betrayed the fact that Billy's mother was already up and preparing to make coffee. Billy shinnied down the ladder from the loft.

"You up too?" Billy's father was by the bedroom door in his long handles, just getting ready to step into his bib overalls. "We must have made enough noise out there to raise the dead."

Mom, in her long nightgown at the hayburner stove, turned and smiled sleepily. "It might have just sounded that way."

"Paw," Billy said, "can I go to town with you this morning?"

Paw was surprised. "What for?"

"Well, I'd just like to."

"Son, I'm not going to be doing a thing but sitting on the porch of the jailhouse."

"That's okay, Paw."

"There won't be any excitement, if that's what you're looking for."

"I'm not. I just thought I'd like to—go along."

Which was true. He had no specific motivation. He hadn't seen much of his father in the past two weeks, and the thought of going to town appealed to him. Possibly, he thought, they could talk about stuff: about McGraw and the hawk and Jeremy and the vigilantes and even Morrie Carson. Billy felt he had things he needed to talk about.

"I won't be any bother," he told his father now.

"Well, it's all right with me if it's all right with your mother."

There had been times when Billy had carried messages

149

like that back and forth from garden to house, or store to wagon, until he thought he was going to go right out of his mind getting one or the other of them to say okay first. In this situation, however, Mom stood right there. She smiled wanly, betraying some worry, but at least didn't pass the buck back.

"You can go, Billy," she said.

Dawn was just breaking over the long mountain range to the east when Billy and his father set out in the wagon for Springer. The air was still and cool. Molly, the mare, moved the wagon along smartly, and they left a pale yellow trail of dust in the air behind them. Meadowlarks sang, in the distance bigger birds soared, and a cottontail sat up and hopped across the road in front of them, comically heading for the cover of the weeds alongside the tire ruts.

"Going to be a pretty one, Billy," Paw said.

"Yes, sir, it sure is."

"Hot, though."

"Looks that way."

"We could use some more rain."

"Yes, sir, we sure could."

"Fourth of July celebration next week. Guess you're looking forward to that."

"Well, I know Maw plans to enter her quilt in the contest."

Paw sighed. "Yes, and I hope she wins. She should. It's a fine quilt. But I don't know, I've tried to warn her—get her ready for it. There's a chance some judges won't vote for her even if her work is the best."

Billy nodded, digesting this. "Because you're a deputy now?"

"That, and not joining the committee."

150

"The vigilantes are just about done by now, though, ain't they, Paw?"

His father grunted. "I'd like to think so."

Ordinarily, the town of Springer was already draped with banners and red, white, and blue bunting this near a Fourth of July celebration. When Billy rode in this morning with his father, however, he saw no signs of preparation at all except for one tattered banner across Main Street and two or three of the fair booths partly constructed in the park. It semed like the town was lying back, not preparing at all as it normally did.

"How come they're not more ready, Paw?" Billy asked.

"I don't know, boy. But I'm not sure I like it."

They went to the jail, which was empty of prisoners at the moment. It smelled musty and sour. Billy got the shutters on the side window open and propped the front door back with a rock, and a dusty little breeze moved through. His father, moving with a curious stiffness, as if the badge on his shirt were sticking him, made coffee and then swept the place out.

"What do we do now?" Billy asked.

"Nothing. If we're lucky."

The town began to awaken. Several men walked past the jail and gave Billy and his father, sitting on the porch, curt nods. A farm wagon drove up to Carson's store in the next block, and a lone horseman rode in. The postmaster came out and washed his window, which he was very proud of. The pinging of the hammer on the anvil and a wisp of dark smoke announced the blacksmith's working day.

Two men left Carson's and walked up the street toward the jail, their feet making tiny puffs in the dirt. Billy recognized them by their stance and their walk, a trick he had learned from observing animals at a great distance. The heavier man was Carson himself, and the other looked like

151

the man who operated a small fix-it shop on the side street; his name was Layden.

Billy's father saw them, of course, at the same time. That was obvious by the way he put down his pipe beside the old rocker. But he didn't say anything. Billy decided to keep his own peace, too.

Carson and Layden walked up to the porch. Carson put his foot on the bottom step. "Morning," he said gruffly.

"Morning, sir," Paw said, with extra politeness. "Morning, Mister Layden."

Layden, a skinny man with one eye that never quite looked in the right direction, took his hands out of his pockets. They were shaking. "Somebody broke into my shop last night."

"Into the fix-it shop?" Paw said more sharply.

"That's right. Two of 'em. Busted the back door in. Took a clock and a watch and most of my tools and eleven dollars cash money, hid in the workbench. And what are you gonna *do* about it?"

"I'll want to go right down there and have a look-see," Paw said, getting to his feet.

"It was done hours ago! What good is you *looking* gonna do?"

Paw's eyes got flinty. "What do you suggest?"

Carson said, "That's why we came. We've decided to try to go along with you—as much as we can."

"That's good news! I—"

"But we know who broke into Joe's place, and we want to know if you're going to go get them, or we have to do it."

"You know who did it? *How?*"

"They was seen," Layden said.

"Someone saw them leave the boarding house empty-handed," Carson said, "and go back a little later with a tow sack."

152

"Where are they now?"

"In the boarding house. Sounded like they got drunk later in the night. They haven't come out this morning. Their horses are still in the livery. We've got the front and back covered, and a man on the roof next door, with a view on their window."

Billy saw his father's face harden. "When you say 'we,' you mean your people."

"I mean the vigilance committee, good citizens willing to do their part for law and order. Right."

"And so far all you've done is watch them?"

"That's right. I told the boys since this is right in Springer, we ought to give you a chance. But I'm warning you. We're moving now, and I consider this a real move toward reconciliation, coming down here and giving you a chance to handle it before we do."

"Well, now," Paw said. "That's very nice of you."

"Are you going down there and get them?"

"That sounds like an ultimatum to me."

Carson made a slashing gesture. "Call it anything you want. I'm giving you a chance. God only knows why. If you don't want it—"

"The fact that two men carried a sack into their room," Paw cut in, "doesn't prove they stole anything."

"What do you think it was? Their family silver? Are you sticking up for them before you've even seen them?"

"I'm telling you the facts."

"They're drifters." Carson looked toward the far block, and the boarding house, with disgust. "Strangers. All they've done in town is idle around and look for trouble."

"Have they caused any trouble?"

"Do you call breaking into this man's shop trouble?"

Paw glanced at Billy and seemed to think about it. The wind stirred along the dusty street. Paw looked like he some-

153

times did toward the end of a long day in the fields. "I'll go talk to them."

"That's not enough. We want them arrested, charged—"

"I'll *talk* to them."

Carson's face, already red, deepened. He controlled himself. "We go with you."

"No."

"We go with you, or we go alone!"

Billy expected his father to argue. For some reason, he didn't. His face settled into even deeper lines. "I'm the constituted law. I talk to them. All you do is observe."

Layden said, "Do we stand here talking all day?"

Paw took a deep breath. "No." He turned and walked into the jail. There was a sound of a chain as he opened the gun cabinet. He came back with a double-barrel shotgun, broken open, and he punched a fat shell into each chamber.

"That's more like it," Carson said, eying the gun.

"I'll *question* them," Paw snapped, and the shotgun clamped shut with a bright metallic ring for emphasis.

His stomach in his mouth, Billy trailed along. They walked up the shady side of the street. His father noticed him when they were almost to the church.

"Billy, you go back."

"Paw!"

"All right. Walk along, then. But when we get to the boarding house, you stand where I tell you. You savvy that?"

Billy nodded quickly, because there was no arguing with that tone.

He did not know what was going to happen, and he did not really know what he *hoped* might happen. A part of his mind saw Paw going in, arresting the men, and being a hero. Another part saw him proving the two were innocent. But over both of these fantasies was this growing, smothering *fear*.

His father, he saw, was all alone. Carson and the others were not really on his side. The men in the boarding house might do anything. And Paw was no lawman. It showed in the way he walked, his shoulders uneven from the work behind the plow, and in the chunks of dirt that kicked up from his heavy shoes—*clodhopper shoes,* people called them sometimes when they wanted to hurt. Paw was not ready for this in any way. None.

But he was going. Billy's mind reeled.

They neared and then reached the boarding house. It had once been a barn or livery, but a few windows had been cut in, a sign hung out front, and two floors built inside. It was not the best boarding house. It looked still more like a barn than anything, and its front was dark in the morning shade.

Standing across the street from the silent front entrance were four men. They had their rifles leaned against the wall of the shed. Seeing them, Billy glanced around quickly and saw another man on down the street, sitting in a wagon, the barrel of his gun bright in the sun. And then Billy looked up and saw the man on the roof of the store building to his right.

Chills filled up on his arms and back.

Carson pointed. "Their room is the first one off the side stairs. Up there."

Following his direction, Billy spotted the doorway to the second floor at the head of some rickety outside stairs that clung to the side wall of the barn. There was a narrow alley there where some dirt that never caught sunlight still looked dark from rain.

Paw was looking up at the staircase. "I'll go up."

155

"We go with you," Carson said.

"*I'll* go up," Paw snapped.

Carson looked at him. "You're a real fool."

Paw's face surprisingly split in a slight grin. "Right."

"You really want to go alone?"

"I do."

Carson stepped back. "Okay, then."

Paw glanced at his shotgun, then around at the other men. He looked up again at the stairs and the door. "Billy, you stay right here."

Billy wanted to say "Yessir," but it didn't come out.

He watched his father walk across the street, test the first step of the old wooden stairs as if unsure, then go up slowly, a step at a time. It was very quiet. Billy could hear the stairs creaking. *Oh Paw,* he thought, *why do you have to do it? Why don't you let them do it? Why are you so dadgummed stubborn?*

He saw his father reach the little landing outside the door, pause, then open the door and go inside. The door closed behind him.

Carson called out softly, but in a voice that carried, "Everybody ready."

The men across the street, and at the other stations, hefted their guns. Carson pulled Billy back to the side, against the shed. "Now you stay put."

From deep inside the boarding house came a muffled shout of some kind. Then—no one would have heard it unless it were this quiet—something hit a wall or a floor, like a piece of furniture falling. Carson, his hands shaking, shaded his eyes as if to see better, although there was nothing to see.

Agonizing moments fled by.

Then the side door—the one on the little landing up there —flew open. A tall, red-haired man incongruously dressed only in baggy long underwear ran out onto the platform, making the whole staircase shudder. He looked confused, sleepy. He looked all around. He had no gun, nothing.

He started down the stairs, three at a time.

Above him, a second man appeared on the landing. He was undressed. He had what looked like a bridle in his left hand.

"That's them!" Carson yelled. "That's them, men!"

The young man in long handles heard the voice and froze in midstride on the stairs, halfway up. He looked around, trying to locate the voice.

On the roof opposite him, the man with a rifle stood. A puff of smoke issued from the muzzle of his weapon, and there was a sharp, clapping, discharge sound. Long handles —Billy would always remember him that way—stood up very straight as he was slammed into the wall.

On all sides the other guns opened up. The explosions crashed together in a single crescendo. Billy saw it all at once—saw the slugs ripping into poor old long handles as he fell, saw the other man, the naked one, freeze in terror and hold up both arms over his head in the gesture of abject surrender, and then saw the first blast of fire take him directly in the face.

Men were running forward, pausing to fire, levering their guns, yelling. A pall of smoke blued the sunlight, and long handles tumbled down the stairs, crashed to the earth, and rolled completely over as more bullets hammered into him. Above, the naked youth stood against the wall, simply nailed there by the continuing impact of heavy-caliber bullets.

Then, by a miracle, it was still. Somebody coughed. A man worked his carbine lever, and a spent shell glittered as it ejected. The naked man tumbled down the steps,

157

hideous and broken. He rolled atop his friend, and lay still.

Billy turned to stare at Paul Carson.

Carson held his gun just as he had held it earlier. He had not fired a shot.

His face was the color of raw dough, and his mouth was open.

A man nearby laughed shrilly. "Looks like we need an undertaker."

"Much lead as they got in 'em," another called, "we might need a winch to pick 'em up."

There was an outburst of laughter that sounded obscene.

Paul Carson continued to watch vacant-eyed. His mouth worked, but no words came out. He looked like a man who had received a mortal blow.

Above, on the landing, the door opened again. Billy's father, his face bloody, staggered out.

Carson made a sound like something dying and rushed forward to help him.

In the doctor's office it was quiet. The doctor expertly taped the bandage on Paw's head. Billy and Paul Carson stood watching. The only sound was the soft tick of an old clock in the corner. Outside, faintly, came the sound of excited voices.

"Listen to them," Carson rasped. *"Celebrating."*

"It was my fault," Paw said. "I got too close when I went into the room. They panicked and I didn't move fast enough. The taller one. He hit me with the lamp, I think."

Carson's eyes were far away. "Celebrating!" he repeated, as if he could not comprehend it.

Paw looked sharply at him. "Well, as it turns out, they were the thieves, you know."

158

Carson's face twisted as if in pain. "What difference does that make?"

"Well, if you want to set an example—"

"Don't," Carson said softly. "Just—don't. All right?"

The two men exchanged looks.

Carson said huskily, "I thought it was the right thing to do. Crime just keeps getting worse. These are good people. You see stores being broken into, drunks along Main Street, even your own son running crazy, refusing to obey—"

"Everybody makes mistakes, Mister Carson."

"But when I saw what they did out there. And then they made *jokes* about it!"

Billy saw his father watching Carson very intently, with an odd glint of compassion in his eyes.

"*Jokes,*" Carson repeated, as if he couldn't believe it.

"You feel different about it now, then."

"What do you think?"

"Then maybe you can shut it down."

"How am I supposed to do that?"

"Aren't you the organizer? People will listen to you."

Carson shuddered. "I'm not in charge. I don't know who is in charge. Chafflin may be in charge. Or White. I don't know. Maybe nobody is in charge."

The doctor finished with the bandaging. "There you are, Baker. Ought to heal fine. Small scar, maybe."

Paw nodded and touched the bandages with his fingertips. He was pale. "I'll pay you just as soon as I can."

Carson said, "I'll pay."

"No."

"I said *I'll pay*. Let me do that much, anyway!"

Billy saw his father consider it soberly. "Mister Carson," he said finally, "I'm very much obliged."

Carson's face was haunted. "I can do that. I don't know what else I can do."

"Maybe this will be the end of it."

Carson did not reply. Even Billy knew his father had spoken to try to make Carson feel better. The end was nowhere in sight.

Stubbornly, because he was that kind of man, Billy's father went back to the jail. He brewed fresh coffee and sat on the porch, the badge on his chest catching the sun now and then. He did not look like a lawman, and seemed to know it.

As the afternoon moved along, the excitement faded and Springer seemed to return near normal.

Later, the Sled family wagon came in. John Sled walked up to the jail. He looked down at his feet as if hesitant to talk, but then raised his head almost defiantly. "We need to talk," he announced.

"Sit down," Billy's father said politely.

"It's about this boy of yours, here. An' Jeremy."

Paw's expression changed slightly—closed. "Go ahead."

Sled hunkered on the porch. "I always say a man ought to live and let live. That's my motto. But sometimes a man has got to speak out on a deal, even if it means riskin' the loss of a friend."

"This is about the hawk, is it?"

"It is. It took me a while, but I finally found out that my boy went up on the mountain yesterday evenin' with your boy, here, and messed around with that crazy man up there."

"He's not crazy," Billy said, "and we didn't mess around. I'm training a hawk, and—"

"Billy," his father said quietly, "shut up."

" 's aw right," Sled said. "I admire the boy for speakin' up. But the fact remains, I don't want my boys goin' up there. I don't want 'em messing around that way. Now

160

I've told Jeremy, an' I wanted to tell you. I expeck Jeremy to obey me. He knows he better. I wanted you to know jus' to be sure your boy, here, gets the message that he ain't to invite Jeremy no more, neither."

"The boys have been walking up there and training a hawk that Billy found, like he said," Dan Baker said. "Billy's been getting back before dark every night; he has his orders about that. I don't think you really have to worry about Jeremy getting into any trouble. They're both good boys. And the old man—"

"Maybe so, maybe so," Sled retorted irritably. "But I jus' don't want Jeremy going up there, that's all! An' that's final!"

Dan Baker drew a slow breath. "You heard the man, Billy."

"Yes, sir," Billy said.

"Has Jeremy gone up there with you often?"

"Once. Yesterday."

"Well, that was the first and last, then. Mister Sled says so. If Jeremy wants to go anyway, you understand that you're to tell him he shouldn't."

"Yes, sir."

Sled said, "If my boy tries to go anyhow, after what I've tole him, I want you to tell your daddy, boy, so he can tell me."

"Well now, just a minute," Dan Baker said. "I'm afraid I won't ask my boy to report on yours that way."

"Why not?" Sled asked heatedly. "If you want to cooperate with a neighbor—"

"I'll ask Billy not to take Jeremy along with him again," Dan Baker said. "But I'll not ask him to report on Jeremy to me or anybody else. They're *friends*, John!"

John Sled's long face went slack. "Well, aw right," he

161

said finally, grudgingly. "But I mean it about Jeremy not going up there. I feel strong about it. Real strong."

"I understand that, John."

"I'll be much obliged to you."

Billy stood with his father and watched the tall, slope-shouldered man walk away, his feet dragging slightly with every step; he left long, light trenches in the dust of the street before each footprint, as if each raising of a shoe was an unthought, massive effort. He shambled across the street to a small crowd on the sidewalk, customary outside the stores at this time of day, and went into one of the shops.

Dan Baker sighed and touched the bandages on his face.

"Why, Paw?" Billy asked.

"I don't know exactly, boy. I guess he wants to—protect Jeremy."

"From McGraw? He wouldn't hurt—"

"No, that's not exactly the way I mean. See, every man wants his son to be like him. But he wants to see his son get farther, too—believe what he does, do what he does, but go farther with it, not have to worry so much, be able to give *his* children a lot more. I know how Jeremy's Dad feels. He figures Jeremy might end up a ne'er-do-well, a tramp. He thinks Jeremy might end up a crazy man on a mountain himself. He worries about it, naturally—"

"That's a funny thing to worry about! I mean it ain't very likely!"

Paw smiled. "Fathers worry about a lot of things, son."

"I guess so!"

"That's why John Sled means business."

A new thought crossed Billy's mind. "Paw, do you worry about *me* like that?"

"I worry about you, yes. Of course."

"I mean—afraid I might be a crazy man some day?"

Paw frowned. "I might."

162

"Then you don't know me at all!"

Paw looked at him thoughtfully. "We've drifted apart lately. Once I thought I knew you well. Now—I'm not sure any more."

It was true, Billy thought with a pang. Since the beginning of this time with the hawk, which was roughly the same as the time since the vigilance committee's first offer, their relationship had been increasingly strained. He didn't feel he knew his father any more.

Desperate for conversation to gloss over this feeling, he said, "I just hope Jeremy ain't too disappointed about not going up there any more."

"You'd better just hope he obeys his dad. If Jeremy keeps going up there against his dad's orders, then Jeremy might not be the only one to suffer."

"Mister Sled wouldn't do anything to McGraw!"

"Wouldn't he?" Paw asked. "In the mood this valley is in right now—wouldn't he?"

Eleven

Springer's July 4 celebration was the quietest on record. People stood around on Main Street under the red-and-white paper bunting and told each other that it was nice, having such a quiet celebration. To Billy, it seemed that the day had no heart in it.

Odd, because the day had all the usual elements. There were the quilting bee, the canning competitions, the baking contest, the pie-eating competition, sack races, speeches, prayers, horse races, horseshoe pitching, wagon decoration prizes, an organ recital at the church, and a band concert late in the afternoon, followed up by a picnic in the park and a square dance. Billy's mother did not win the quilting bee. Otherwise, the day went about as it might have been predicted, with the first child—a boy belonging to the Dodges—throwing up a little before noon, and the last barrel going empty a little after dark, at a point when several wives were already making serious threats about future actions if their men persisted in staying any longer.

To Billy, it just seemed a little forced this year. Possibly he felt this way because he knew his parents were forcing their gaiety somewhat, and Jeremy was, too.

Jeremy was obeying his father and not going back up the mountain. He was depressed about it. He and his father had not argued over it because it would never have occurred to Jeremy to seriously question an order like that. But he didn't like it.

"Did you tell Mister McGraw I'm sorry?" he asked Billy for the tenth time at the town celebration.

"I told him," Billy assured him, "and he said you're sure welcome to visit later any time, if things straighten out."

"I don't know if they ever will," Jeremy said despairingly.

"They will, Jeremy. I mean, look at how it's quieted down around town the past few days. Since them two guys got shot messing with my paw at the jail, there hasn't been *any* rough stuff. Your paw will calm down and stop worrying so much, and then you can come back up to see my hawk at Mister McGraw's again sometime soon."

Each day, Jeremy got by Billy's house at some time and asked for a report on the training of the hawk. Billy told him carefully each time, in detail, torn between his own enthusiasm and the fear of seeming to boast. Each day, it seemed, he had new information and a new phase to talk about.

The day was fast approaching when Billy and the hawk had to meet the ultimate test: free flight. Each day's work took them closer to it now.

The hawk was learning fast with the lure, the leather object fitted with feathers and a lead cord. At first it had been used only as it was that first time Billy and Jeremy had witnessed it: Food had been attached so that the hawk had to "attack" it on the ground in front of him in order to eat. Quickly, however, McGraw had moved along to teasing the hawk with the lure, jerking it along the ground so the hawk had to pounce, and then a few days ago the flight work had begun.

The hawk's exercise on the long tether line and its feeding with the lure were brought together now in this latest phase of work. The lure—sure to get the hawk's attention now, and no longer holding food as an attachment—was swung aloft on a cord; the hawk was allowed to fly on his tether cord. From the first time this was done, the hawk veered from his usual straight flight and attacked the lure. Now McGraw swung the lure and Billy tossed the hawk; the hawk flew wild patterns trying to catch the lure as McGraw swung it in odd-shaped trajectories, making the hawk work for it. McGraw always let the hawk catch the lure eventually, and there was always a strip of raw meat as a reward. While the hawk chased the lure, Billy blew the small whistle, so that hopefully one day soon the hawk would respond to the whistle as a signal to return, even when the lure was not in evidence.

This was a little more difficult. For the past two evenings, as part of the work, they had tossed the hawk and tried to get it to veer back for return solely on the basis of the whistle being sounded. The hawk, each time, had kept right on going to the end of its line as if nothing were being done.

"The dummy's never going to get it!" Billy had said in exasperation.

"He'll get it, he'll get it," McGraw said patiently.

"You can't be sure," Billy had protested. "You can't *know*. I mean, sometimes a hawk will go just so far, and then just stop learning, right?"

"Granted, sonny. But not this hawk. This hawk likes you too much. Look at him right now, setting there, his head cocked, watching for you. He's practically grinning. I've

166

never seen a hawk like a person the way this hawk likes you. That's why he'll keep learning for you."

"I wish you'd tell *him* that, then, so he'd go ahead and obey this whistle!"

McGraw just chuckled.

He seemed little affected, McGraw did, by the news from town. He had been dismayed to hear Jeremy couldn't come back any more, although the news hadn't seemed to surprise him. And as for Billy's recital of facts about the vigilance committee checking into people's backgrounds, McGraw had said nothing at all; he'd merely shrugged and looked a shade glum.

"You know," Billy had told him finally, driven to candor, "those folks could get after *you.*"

McGraw, cutting up some beef strips to feed the hawk, said nothing.

"If you got anything in your background, that is, that they might not like," Billy added, fishing.

McGraw still said nothing.

"Well?" Billy said.

"I'll tell you something about dealing with people, sonny," McGraw said at last, straightening up and thoughtfully patting his ample belly. "You've got to act like they're going to be rational."

"Does 'rational' mean good sense?"

"More or less, yes."

"Yeah, but people *ain't* always rason—uh—what you said."

"I know," McGraw sighed.

"Then what do you do when you count on 'em to be, and they're not?"

"You adjust, sonny. You adjust."

It was just one of three or four times Billy made a strenuous attempt to get McGraw excited about his own potential

167

danger, or to determine what McGraw's background really was. McGraw refused to get excited about anything. As for his background, he might as well have come out of the rocks, like the wild creatures he befriended. He seemed to have no past, and he liked it that way.

Billy tried to probe his background.

In the shed one evening:

"You sure know a lot about hawks."

"You live and learn, sonny."

"A lot of hawks around where you grew up?"

"Oh, some."

"Where *did* you grow up, anyhow?"

Silence.

While training the hawk:

"You suppose they ever used hawks to carry messages?"

"I doubt it, boy. A hawk will hunt and retrieve, but carrying a message—that's asking a lot of loyalty for a hawk."

"They use pigeons to carry messages, though, right?"

"In the Army, yes."

"Were you ever in the Army?"

Silence.

Cutting meat:

"Boy, it's hot today!"

"Sure is."

"Was it this hot where you grew up?"

Silence.

Sitting in the cliff shade, resting:

"I guess you never had any family of your own."

Silence.

There was simply no way McGraw could be cajoled, tricked, or taunted into revealing anything of himself in terms of the past. Whether he had things better left forgotten, or was merely a private person, Billy could only

168

guess. Worried as he was about the vigilance committee, he consistently imagined the worst: McGraw was wanted for a crime somewhere; or McGraw actually did have crazy moments, and had to be put away periodically; or McGraw had run off from a wife and six children; or McGraw had escaped from prison.

Theories such as these were hard to square with experience, however. McGraw had to be the kindest, gentlest man in the world.

And if there was anything he did not know about hawks, Billy was not even interested in knowing about it either. McGraw seemed to know every move old Melvin—he called the hawk this every once in a while, just for a joke—was going to make before he even made it. The hawk still surprised and amazed Billy consistently. McGraw never seemed surprised.

They had begun calling the hawk "her" at least part of the time. That was because McGraw had thought it was a female, possibly. He had explained that females got a lot bigger, half-again as big sometimes, and Billy's hawk seemed to have some fat on its bones for growth potential even despite its deprived youth as the runt of the nest.

Lately, though, it had all been "him" or "Melvin." This had not been discussed. Billy knew it meant the old man was sure, now, that this hawk was a male. So it would be a slightly smaller hawk. But Billy saw no reason to think this was bad. *No* hawk could have been better, really, even a larger female.

"We're coming right along with this ole hawk," Billy said once.

"Yes, sir, we are at that," McGraw agreed.

"I think this hawk likes me."

"Yes, sir."

"He likes you too, of course, but he does like me. Don't you think?"

McGraw smiled. "I think he likes you."

"That might mean I'm a good person, if he likes me and I can man him."

"Billy, you're a good person whether a hawk sees it or not. I want you to remember that."

Billy thought about it, and the thoughts felt good.

"Mister McGraw?"

"Yes, sonny?"

"Don't you ever get lonesome up here by yourself?"

"I used to," McGraw said with a smile, "before you started coming."

"If I stopped coming, what would you do?"

"Why, be lonesome again, I reckon."

"Would you move to town, to be around people?"

"No, sir, I wouldn't."

"Why do you like to live alone the way you do?"

"Sonny, some men are like some animals; they have to live in a pack. Others are like other creatures; they have to stay alone. That's the way nature set us up, and if we're ever going to be happy, we have to learn to be true to our own nature, and not fight the way we are."

"People get worried about hermits and such," Billy pointed out.

"Animals that run in packs always get nervous about ones that travel alone—unless the one alone is a doe or something helpless."

"I guess if you're going to stay out of the pack, you'd better be as strong as you can."

"I guess so, youngster."

"And not be afraid."

"And control the fear. The man who said he wasn't ever afraid was the biggest liar the Good Lord ever created."

170

"Are you ever afraid?"

"Of course I am, sonny."

"When?"

"Why—lots of times. Every day, I suppose, in one way or another."

"What are you afraid of?"

McGraw's face lined more heavily with serious thought. "Of getting hurt. Of dying. Of being chased. Of everything staying the same. Of everything changing too fast. Of living too long or not long enough, or getting too lonesome or having too much company. Of being misunderstood or being understood too well. Of being hated. Of being loved."

"Do you think a lot of people in town hate you?"

"I don't know, sonny. What do you think?"

"I don't think they hate you, but I think they're afraid of you, some."

"You may be right. I made some bread. Come see if you like it."

During the week or so following July 4, Billy made it to McGraw's every afternoon, and the training of the hawk went along swiftly. In town, as far as Billy knew, things were quiet. The re-election campaign of Ad Sweeney was in full swing. He had three opponents: two members of the vigilance group in Springer and a bar owner from Rawson Pass. There had been two nights when distant fires stained the horizon, and Billy's father rode out to return many hours later, gaunt and bitter-eyed. The vigilantes had located just about all of those they didn't approve, Paw said. He did not elaborate. It seemed the kind of thing Billy did not want to pursue too diligently. Maybe he didn't really want to know.

On a Tuesday night, Billy was intercepted by Morrie Carson again. This time Morrie had only one companion, Robertson. They had been fishing, and each had a stringer

171

of good trout. The good luck hadn't improved Morrie's temper any.

"Out again by yourself?" he grunted. "I thought we told you it would be a whole lot smarter for you to stay close to home."

"I was jus' walking," Billy said. He had his back to the slope of a gully, the countryside around was heavy with wild berry bushes that made running impossible, and both Morrie and Robertson were mounted. "Didn't think it would hurt to walk, Morrie."

"Don't try to smart-mouth me," Morrie said, making a move as if to dismount.

"Leave him alone, Morrie," Robertson said weakly.

Morrie turned in the saddle to glare at his buddy. "What was that?"

Robertson looked down, and his weak jaw trembled. "I said, leave him alone. Please. He's not bothering anyone."

"You're not trying to order me, though," Morrie said intently. It was very important to Morrie that nobody order him. He seemed to burn up a tremendous amount of energy making sure what people thought of him, and assuring himself that they weren't taking advantage of him in some way.

Robertson, however, was essentially so weak that it took little threat for him to knuckle under. He knuckled under now. "No, Morrie, I sure wasn't trying to order you."

Morrie turned back to Billy. "I don't want to catch you out here again."

"You're telling me to stay home?" Billy said, incredulous.

"I don't want to see you out here," Morrie repeated.

"What makes you think you can boss anybody like that?"

Morrie grinned and balled a big fist. *"This* does, kid."

The incident worried Billy, naturally. But there was

172

about as much chance of him stopping his trips now as there was of the sun coming up in the west. He figured out a way to start down the road as if he was going to town, then get into the woods beside Dead Man's Hill so *nobody* could observe him the rest of the way. He didn't tell his father about the incident because he was afraid it might raise questions about continued visits.

A day or so after Morrie stopped him, Billy got home to find Jeremy waiting for him. This was not unusual, but Jeremy's air of controlled excitement was.

"I've got me a hawk of my own," he told Billy in the privacy of the garden.

"Where?" Billy asked. "How? A red-tail?"

"It's not a red-tail, and I don't know what kind it is. It's got a yellow beak and yellow eyes. It's smaller'n yours. It flew in our barn. It got hurt. It can't fly. I've got it hid out in the crik bottom, in a crate."

"Is it gonna live? Are you gonna be able to feed it, and all?"

Jeremy's long face got longer. "I don't know."

"You'll have to give it water, and get you some raw meat. Cut it in thin strips. You saw how we did for my hawk."

"I'll do what I can, but—could you come down and have a look at it?"

"I'll have to come after supper," Billy decided, checking the low sun.

"Jus' come out back, down in the crik there. Okay? That way you won't haf to ask anybody at the house and let my daddy know, or nothing like that."

"I don't suppose your daddy would approve, huh?"

"He'd kill it," Jeremy said somberly.

Billy did not let on at his own supper table, listening to his parents talk about the crops, the need for more rain, and the political situation in Springer. Afterward, he slipped out and found Jeremy in the creek bottom.

The hawk, housed in a crate fixed with a piece of an old blanket, was a kind Billy had never seen before, either. In addition to yellow bill and eyes, it had yellow feathers in its wings and a pure white body. It was about fourteen inches long, making it almost a third smaller than his red-tail.

It was one extremely scared hawk, and its wing seemed to be badly beaten up. It wouldn't eat. Jeremy was sort of pitiful about it, excited and proud, but worried sick at the same time. Billy told him everything probably would be fine, but he was not sure of that at all. The hawk was going to die fast if it refused to eat.

The next afternoon, McGraw wasn't very encouraging. He agreed with Billy's diagnosis, judging by his description, and said he was worried not only about the hawk, but about how Jeremy would take it if he lost the thing. There was also something else on McGraw's mind, and for once Billy managed to pry it out of him. Some pranksters had been around in the night, throwing empty cans down off the cliff and shooting into the clearing. The cans were just nuisance and the bullets were intended as the same, McGraw said, although the trouble was that a stray slug might bounce in any direction and hurt something or somebody. Billy said he had half a mind to tell his father about it, but McGraw said if things ran true to form, the pranksters wouldn't be back for three or four months again, and let sleeping dogs lie.

Getting home by his new, circuitous route to avoid any possible meeting with Morrie Carson or his friends, Billy found Jeremy waiting for him again.

"He's worse," Jeremy said, wringing his hands. "He's *real*

174

worse, Billy, he's *bad*. He's getting weak. He won't make it. I've gotta do something to save him!"

"Do you think you could let him go? He might make it on his own, I mean, at least he might try to eat, not be so scared—"

Jeremy shook his head. "That's not it. There's only one chance. I'm gonna take it. I mean it. I've got to. You've got to help me, too. Tomorrow. You've got to."

"Help you do what?" Billy thought he already knew.

"I've got to take that little hawk up to the old man," Jeremy said. "Just the way you did with yours. It's the only chance that little bird is gonna *have*."

"Your paw will take your hide off," Billy pointed out.

"Are you gonna tell him?"

"Of course not!"

"Then you'll help me get my hawk up there tomorrow?"

Billy thought about it. "Yes," he said finally.

He knew he was taking a chance. He just didn't know how much a chance it was.

In the morning the leaden sky dripped a steady, bleak mist. It made work on the farm impossible, but Billy figured it might be the luckiest thing that had ever happened to Jeremy's small hawk. Finishing his inside chores as quickly as he dared without raising obvious questions about his unusual efficiency, Billy hightailed down the road to the Sled farm.

The misting rain had already made the road a red slime, and by the time Billy had gotten to the neighboring farm he was beginning to wonder if there was really much chance of climbing to McGraw's place before the weather broke. One look at Jeremy's face settled that issue.

"He didn't eat anything, Billy, and he's just layin' in the box out there, hardly moving or anything. I got some stuff to put over it so's he won't get wet, but he's bound to be cold, and he's so weak, he just sorta rolls his eyes a little, that's all. He's dyin', Billy."

"Well, he ain't going to die," Billy said with a lot more confidence than he actually felt. "We'll just git him up to Mister McGraw; he'll know what to do."

"When can we go?"

"What's wrong with right now?"

Jeremy cast a worried glance toward the embankment that hid his hawk. Then he turned and looked at the house. "My daddy's inside."

"Well, look, Jeremy. If you're too worried to go, that's all right. I think I can get your hawk up there okay. I got mine up there by myself, and it was bigger than yours."

Jeremy's jaw set. "No, sir. It's my hawk. I'll go with you."

So they set out. It was no big problem, slipping down to the gully behind the Sled place and collecting the box, which Jeremy had wrapped as best he could in some oiled paper and a piece of old canvas. They headed out northwest, staying to the creek bottom, moving as fast as they could carry the box without jostling the hawk to death in the process.

By the time they had gone a mile, Jeremy was as wet as Billy was, which was saying plenty. The rich red Colorado dirt stuck heavily to their boots, making the going progressively harder. Jeremy kept glancing back, as if expecting to see his father coming after him. Billy felt sorry for him, and didn't make matters any worse by mentioning the previous run-ins with Morrie Carson. On a miserable day like this, he thought, Morrie and his buddies would stay in anyway.

The rain thinned, but seemed to get colder, as they worked their way across the rougher, higher land north of

176

Springer. They could look down from this vantage point ordinarily and see the entire valley, but today they couldn't even see the town. Deep gray haze masked everything, and isolated them on the side of the old mountain as if they, and their sick hawk, were the only creatures remaining in the world.

Taking his turn carrying the box that contained Jeremy's injured hawk, Billy noticed what he considered an ominous thing: Even when he happened to tip the box a little, there was no movement within—no sign that the hawk was alarmed by the jostling, or was moving around to try to stay in an upright position. Billy was not about to mention this to Jeremy, who already seemed more worried than ever, but it did prey on his own mind.

Partway up the mountain the weather began to change rapidly. At first they thought they were getting above low clouds, but then it became apparent that the clouds were thinning on all sides. The mist slacked and stopped. Where there had been no wind of any kind, now a brisk, cool one developed quickly, making Billy shiver as his clothes dried. The sun broke completely through the overcast, and a huge rainbow formed across the western end of the valley. It was going to become a clear, cool mountain day.

Working up through the band of evergreen forest that led to McGraw's retreat, Billy and Jeremy made better time. They got out of the woods and looked up the last slope to the cliffhouse and outbuildings. A wisp of woodsmoke blued the clearing air, most of it issuing from the fat black pipe that protruded at an angle from the front of McGraw's house.

"Mister McGraw!" Billy called, hurrying up the final slope ahead of Jeremy.

A voice *behind* him, in the woods, called quietly, "No need to yell, Billy boy."

Billy turned, and there was McGraw, coming out of deep brush. He walked bent over, like a man carrying a tent, which he virtually was. He had a heavy canvas draped over him for shelter, and its edges dragged the ground as he came toward them.

"What've you been doing?" Billy demanded. "Trying to catch you something?"

McGraw smiled grimly. "Some*body* would be more like it."

Billy saw for the first time how tired the older man looked, and how his clothes, despite the tarp, were dark, soaked through. McGraw was pale, and Billy was shocked to see a bluish tinge to his lips.

"They've been back?" Billy guessed.

"Afraid so," McGraw muttered. He dismissed the entire subject with a weary glance at Jeremy. "Glad to see you again, youngster. Your daddy had a change of heart?"

"Not exactly," Jeremy flushed. But then his jaw set again in that stubborn way of his. "I've got something—a hawk." He put the crate down on the ground in front of McGraw.

"A hawk, is it? Well, now, is it like Billy's?"

"No, it's a different kind, and I don't know what kind, and it's sick," Jeremy said in a rush. "It's *real* sick, Mister McGraw. The only thing I could think to do was bring it up here to you."

"Well, now," McGraw said softly, squatting to remove the canvas from the box on the wet earth. "I guess we'd better see what we can see, then, hadn't we."

Jeremy nodded mutely, and McGraw carefully removed the oiled paper from the box lid and cautiously opened it.

Jeremy leaned past Billy to look in over McGraw's shoulder, and saw first. "*Aw*," he said huskily, as if he had been hurt.

McGraw knelt in the wet dirt, looking into the box.

Jeremy turned to Billy, his eyes mirrorlike with surprise and pain. He did not say anything, but his jaw worked and his lips turned down at the corners, and then his eyes changed again, filled.

"I'm afraid we started a little late, youngster," McGraw said regretfully.

"He was just a little guy," Jeremy choked.

"Well," McGraw murmured, examining the body of the small hawk with tender hands, "he'd had a bad accident, Jeremy—see how his wing is hurt here? And his breast, too, like he hit something real, real hard. He was too badly hurt to save."

Jeremy just stood there, the size of a man with tears running down his little-boy face. He didn't say anything.

"If we had managed to save his life," McGraw added, "he would have been a cripple. He couldn't have flown again, not after that injury. He had taken an *awful* whack."

Jeremy nodded, but kept looking off at the woods. He didn't want them to see his tears, Billy guessed.

McGraw's forehead wrinkled massively. He licked his lips and seemed to make at least two false starts at saying something. Then he made another try.

"I had a pet kitten," he said softly. "I called her Sheba. She was little. She got sick. I did everything I could, but sometimes there just isn't enough you *can* do. I buried little old Sheba back there behind the sheds, beside the cottonwood. It's a real nice spot. You get shade and you can hear the creek real nice."

Jeremy said nothing, just kept crying silently.

McGraw asked gently, "Would you like to bury your hawk back there?"

"Yes, sir, I guess I would."

There was a silence. It might not have been so bad for Jeremy, Billy thought, if he had ever had many pets before,

179

or if his father hadn't told him not to come back up the mountain. Jeremy had risked just about everything, and now he had nothing to show for it. What made it worse, Billy guessed, was that it had to be a lot harder to take an all-out risk a second time—after the first such risk hadn't gotten you a thing except the fear that went with it.

With the silence dragging out, McGraw asked softly, "Would you like some help burying him, Jeremy?"

Jeremy squared his skinny shoulders. "No. I'll do it just fine."

"The spade is beside the bigger shed."

For an instant Billy felt a rush of wild rage like he had never felt before; he wanted to strike at McGraw with both fists, beating him in the face for his uncharacteristic callousness. Why was he pushing Jeremy this way? What was the awful rush about getting the dead hawk into the ground? Why didn't McGraw leave Jeremy *alone* for a little while—even for a few minutes?

Jeremy, however, responded with no such obvious emotion. Woodenly he picked up the crate containing his dead hawk and started for the shed. His muddy feet dragged tiredly, but as he walked, he seemed to move with more determination.

Which was when Billy got it: You had to go ahead and *do* something when it hurt like this, and McGraw knew it. What seemed callousness was kindness. He was not going to let Jeremy stand around and grieve.

McGraw asked Billy softly now, "Do you think he runs any more risk of trouble with his daddy if he stays around here a while this morning?"

"I don't know why he would, sir. His paw sure won't follow him up here, and I really don't think anybody seen us go."

McGraw nodded soberly. "In that case, then, I think we

180

ought to give your friend something to think about. You're here anyway. Let's fly your hawk and give Jeremy a job to do to help us with it."

"Do you think that's what we really ought to do?" Billy asked dubiously.

"Yes, sir," McGraw said with great dignity. "I do."

By the time Jeremy had come back from his job with the shovel behind the shed, Billy and McGraw had the red-tail out and waiting for its morning's work. The earlier misty rain had all burned away now, and a brilliant sunlight flooded the hillside fronting McGraw's cliff dwelling. Billy's hawk sat his perch handsomely, the slight, high breeze riffling his feathers, his head fiercely erect and alert. Jeremy got an oddly stricken expression as he walked partway from the sheds to the cleared slope where Billy and McGraw were playing out exercise cords and readying the lure.

McGraw turned to Jeremy with a matter-of-fact expression. "Will you help us do some of this work with Baker's hawk?"

Jeremy looked at Billy and then at the hawk. "Sure," he said firmly.

They prepared. The exercise line was played out and recoiled loosely near the hawk's perch. The lure string was played out. Billy had the whistle and the glove ready. McGraw carefully paced off directions to make sure they would not provide the hawk enough line to make it into an awkward situation. One day they had miscalculated, allowing the hawk extra line in the direction of the woods. Billy hadn't been able to make it up the pine tree; McGraw, sweating and muttering about an old man's stupidity, had had to get the hawk down.

"You still haven't told us what happened to make you

181

spend part of the night in the woods," Billy pointed out to McGraw.

McGraw shrugged and reacted as if Billy had asked him something about his background. "Nothing unusual. Jeremy, do you want to bring that lure over here, please?"

The way McGraw set it up, he was to toss the hawk, Billy was to whistle and lure it, and Jeremy was to bring it back if and when it failed to take the lure and instead flew to the end of its cord and landed. The morning had become crystal and beautiful, and the hawk seemed to sense Billy's eagerness. The large bird moved restlessly on its perch, rattling the light brass swivels.

Billy began swinging the lure, making sure the hawk saw it. McGraw held the hawk on the glove near the center perch, being patient and making sure it understood what was going on. Jeremy hurried to the edge of the rocks off to the right; his eyes had come partly alive again, and Billy thought the exercise might help him get through his grief.

"Everybody ready?" McGraw asked.

"Ready!" Billy said, swinging the lure.

McGraw tossed the hawk. It flapped its wings eagerly and ignored the lure and Billy's piping whistle to fly straight and steady toward the woods. It caught on the end of the line and fluttered to the ground.

"Dummy!" Billy yelled, letting the lure swing to the earth.

"Let him get that one out of his system," McGraw smiled. "Now he'll be ready to play the game right. You going to get him, Jeremy?"

Jeremy was already hurrying over to the spot where the hawk had landed. He had the second glove, a lightweight model made by McGraw for carrying, and as he held his arm down in front of the hawk, it hopped obediently up to be carried.

"Good boy!" McGraw called. "Bring him back, now."

Jeremy returned the hawk to McGraw's larger glove.

"I think he'll do the right thing this time," McGraw said easily, holding the bird in tossing position. "You ready, Billy?"

Billy began swinging the lure in a wide arc, lengthening the cord as centrifugal force took the lure farther and higher, out twenty feet or more from his body. "Yes!" he called. "Ready!"

McGraw tossed again. The hawk started for the trees once more. Furious, Billy blew hard on the small wooden whistle, puffing his cheeks out and hurting them. The hawk veered slightly in his flight, banked upward, its spread wings making a hard curvature against the painfully blue sky, and then coming on over as it swung over the top, inverting and diving for the lure as it swung around its tight little arc. The hawk made no corrections that could be detected by the eye in its flight path; it swung up and around and down again, wings canting backward, talons jutting forward. As quick as light it struck the lure. Both lines—the hawk's and the lure's—went slack and became crazy coils in the air. The hawk bore the lure instantly to the ground practically at Billy's feet.

"That's the boy!" Billy yelped. "That's more like it!"

"He's learning," McGraw chuckled, walking over to retrieve the bird.

"If that'd been a real bird," Jeremy enthused, "it wouldn't have had a chance!"

The work was helping him forget his own bird. Billy winked at him. "Let me do it a few more times, and maybe you can try swinging the lure."

"*Boy!* Could I?"

They both looked at McGraw.

"No reason why not," he shrugged. He knelt to pick the hawk up again.

Jeremy hurried to the rocks to be on station for the next toss.

Which was a failure. The hawk ignored the lure and whistle, just as if the second try had not been so perfect, and went straight for the trees again. Billy's bawl of disappointment followed it to the end of the tether line and then down its awkward little fluttering descent to the gravel only a few paces from the brush that bordered heavier woods.

"Well," McGraw frowned, "he's awful feisty today. Never saw him act so strange."

Jeremy hustled over toward the bird.

The brush near the hawk became the scene of a commotion, and then it parted and two figures stepped out into the clearing.

They came out so quickly, yet so casually, that Billy for a moment could not quite understand what was going on. He saw it all at once: Jeremy stop in midstride and stare in surprise; the two young men stride out and stand there, legs spread, grins cocky over the surprise they knew they had provided; the hawk ruffle its feathers and stand nervously not far from where they had emerged; and McGraw stiffen from head to foot, his face becoming a thunderhead.

The intruder was Morrie Carson, and his companion was Robertson.

In the space of a second or two, several things clicked into focus for Billy. He knew from McGraw's expression that Morrie and Robertson must be the two who had caused a commotion in the night, harassing the older man; now Morrie looked very pleased with himself because he felt so much in command, and he was neither a man nor a boy, but moving toward manhood with every passing moment—with the realization of his power over the present situation.

The two young men had been out much of the night;

184

that much was obvious from their dark-soaked hats and jackets, tied on the saddles of the horses, which Robertson now led into view from the woods. Morrie had a rifle in his hands, and both he and his companion wore a revolver on the right hip. They looked tired, worn from a hunt, but vibrantly alive again now with renewed excitement. That strange light had never been half so bright in Morrie's eyes.

"What'd you do, old man?" he called laconically. "Send for help?"

"You two better just get out of here," McGraw said. "These boys and I are minding our own business."

Morrie's lip turned down. "What're you going to do, old man? Have Billy tell his old man?"

Robertson giggled and recled slightly. "Some deputy! Vigilantes have to save his skin for him."

He was a little drunk, Robertson was, and Billy, as he saw this, also realized that Morrie was in the same shape. It struck a chill into him. While it helped explain why they had harassed McGraw for no reason beyond a general prejudice, it also made this moment infinitely less predictable and dangerous. A sober Morrie might have given trouble, but would have drawn the line short of real violence. Drunk, either of them might do anything.

"Yeah," Morrie grinned now. "Your daddy won't save you, Billy boy."

Jeremy sang out, "You guys leave him alone."

Morrie turned mocking at Jeremy, who was his own height, but whose younger age was given away in the slenderness of his build. "Listen, Sled, I happen to know *your* daddy told you not to be up in these parts. You're in plenty of trouble already, without shooting off your face."

"That's my business," Jeremy said stoutly.

While this had been going on, Billy's hawk had remained on the ground between the contending sides. Now, closer to

185

Morrie and Robertson, it evidenced its nervousness in this new situation by unfolding its great wings and moving about a few inches on the ground.

"You *playing* with this ugly thing?" Morrie asked.

"Training him," Billy shot back.

Morrie looked at Robertson. "Want to have some more fun?"

McGraw took a step forward and pointed a stubby finger. "This is your last warning, boys. I'm using this property, and you two had better get out of here."

It was so obviously an empty threat that Billy's insides sank. Morrie grinned. The rifle over his arm was aimed in McGraw's general direction with a casualness that was more frightening than more careful handling might have been. "What did you say, old man?"

"You heard me," McGraw said. He did not, amazingly, look frightened. "You boys are going to get yourself into more trouble than you can handle."

"You talk real big."

Jeremy started toward the hawk—which was also toward Morrie and Robertson.

"What're you doing?" Robertson snapped nervously.

"I'm getting the hawk."

"No, you're not," Morrie said. "You just stay right where you are."

"I'll get it," McGraw muttered, and took a step.

"Hold it," Morrie said.

The rifle now pointed at McGraw's chest, and whatever light lived in Morrie's eyes was a dancing flame. McGraw froze in his tracks.

"What're you *doing* this for?" Billy cried. "Why don't you get *outta* here, like he said?"

"I don't like you, Billy boy," Morrie said quietly. "And I don't like this clumsy, freaky clodhopper"—nodding to-

186

ward Jeremy—"and I don't like *him*," his eyes returning to McGraw.

Jeremy cried, "He ain't hurt you none!"

"Living by hisself," Morrie said, "actin' so high an' mighty, like he's too good for ordinary folks. He's just like Billy boy, with his stupid pet animals. A man don't mess with animals like that. He does his work. He keeps his nose on the grindstone. He don't have time for lordin' it over folks or playin' around like a stupid idjit."

The hawk, becoming increasingly restive, opened its wings again and moved around on the ground in a little circle, dragging its swivels and line.

Morrie watched the hawk an instant, then shrugged and brightened. "Although I guess we shouldn't complain, huh, Robertson? We sure wouldn't have had such a good dinner last night if that meat hadn't been so tame."

Robertson grinned blearily. "Wisht I had more easy shots like that."

"What are you talking about?" McGraw asked.

"Our supper las' night," Morrie said, the light brighter and wilder. "We was down on the slope. This little ole deer come out of the cover. Bobby, here, started to snap a shot, but that little ole deer made it downright easy for us. She walked right up to us, practically, like she expected a handout or something. Funniest thing I ever did see."

Billy, suddenly sick at his stomach, looked at McGraw. The man's face sloped downward, and then seemed to start to go to pieces. "You didn't shoot that fawn!"

"See?" Robertson said. "I *told* you he'd probably tamed the durned thing! You don't have an animal walk right up to your gun like that unless it's been tamed by somebody."

Morrie was watching McGraw, and his face showed the pleasure he was deriving from the obvious pain in the

187

older man's expression. "Sure was tasty meat, though, irregardless."

"You cowards!" Billy screamed. "You rotten, no-'count *cowards!* You better git outta here right now, an' stay out, or my paw *will* throw you in jail!"

Morrie grinned. "Right, Billy boy. We'll leave. If that's what you want, you snot-nose little punk, with your snooty ways."

Putting the rifle in his left hand, he stepped forward, heading toward the hawk.

"Stay away from him!" Billy yelled.

Morrie ignored him, and bent over the hawk, which pranced and moved nervously at being approached in this new and threatening way. "We'll just have some fun with your bird, here, first—"

"*Stop it!*"

Morrie reached down and grabbed the hawk by the legs. He swung it up as one might swing up a helpless chicken about to be tossed down onto a chopping block. The hawk screamed and its wings exploded in terror and fury. Morrie yelled something angrily, surprised, and dropped the rifle to try to grab the hawk with the other hand. Billy, thinking the hawk was being torn apart, ran forward.

At that moment, Morrie lost his grip.

The hawk turned over in the air at the level of his waist and got its wings straightened out for flight. It shot upward a dozen feet, black for the smallest fraction of an instant against the sky. Morrie staggered backward a step. Robertson's face was agape. The hawk swung in the air in the same moment and turned—*not* toward the woods, or toward its perch or toward seeming freedom—

It dived on Morrie.

At the last second of the brief dive, it rotated its wings and body so that talons lashed down into his face.

188

The talons dug, red spurted, the wings beat a mad rhythm, Morrie flailed his arms, started to fall, and screamed. The hawk broke free, described a blindingly swift arc low to the ground, and landed almost at Billy's feet.

Morrie screamed again with the pain, and fell.

Twelve

With Morrie Carson thrashing on the ground, bubbling sounds coming from his throat, McGraw rushed toward him. Robertson, pale with panic, raised the rifle.

"No closer, old man!"

"I want to try to help him!" McGraw ignored the rifle and knelt beside Morrie. "Here, let me look—"

But Morrie shoved McGraw's hands away furiously and struggled unsteadily to his feet. All the blood was on the lower portion of his jaws, and on his throat. He whipped out a bandana and pressed it against his wounds, motioning frantically at Robertson with his other hand. "Let's get to town—to the doc!"

"I'll help you here first," McGraw argued. "Let me at least make sure there aren't any veins punctured—"

Morrie swung into the saddle, and his horse staggered in a half circle. Dazed, bleeding around his hands and the bandana, the youth raised a fist. "I'll get you for this, old man! And you wait, Billy!"

Further words were cut off as the horse swung on around and Morrie caught the reins, touching his spurs at the same instant. The horse exploded into violent forward movement,

190

dirt and pebbles being spewed from its hooves. As Morrie's horse charged into the brush, Robertson got into the saddle and hurried after him, leaving the rifle on the ground in his haste.

Billy felt rooted to the spot as he and his companions listened to the thrashing of the horses fade and then vanish in the woods down the mountain somewhere.

Jeremy recovered first. He hurried across the clearing and picked up the rifle. "They forgot this. It serves them right." He turned to McGraw. "It's yours now—"

"No," McGraw replied sharply. "Put it down, youngster."

"But it's a fine gun, and I—"

"Put it down!"

McGraw's words were so sharp that Jeremy, stricken, dropped the rifle.

McGraw raised his hands and pressed fingertips against his temples. "I don't know how badly hurt that lad might be. Your hawk struck back, Billy!"

"I can't say I'm exactly sorry."

"I know," McGraw replied sadly, looking down at the hawk, now calm, as if nothing had happened. "No wild creature is ever truly safe. The boy was going to hurt it —you could see that. The hawk knew it too."

Billy took the glove from the older man and bent to pick up his hawk, which obediently hopped up onto his arm the moment he offered it. Billy held the hawk out to the side so it would look at McGraw and give him a chance to look directly at its wings and body, to see if there was any injury. He couldn't see anything at all. The hawk moved nervously on the glove.

"We'd better put him in the shed," McGraw said.

They walked to the shed, put the hawk on its interior perch, and went back outside again. Only then, standing there in the vast, morning silence, did Billy begin to realize what had happened.

"They'll get to town inside an hour," he said. "They'll raise the biggest commotion anybody ever saw."

Jeremy said, "They can't say what happened. He was hurting the hawk!"

"Do you think Morrie, or Robertson either, will tell *the truth?*" Billy asked.

Jeremy's eyes widened as he thought about it. "If they don't, it'll sound like—they make it sound like—"

"—like my hawk attacked him for no reason," Billy supplied bitterly.

"If he does that, somebody else could come up here and try to kill the hawk!"

"Now, wait a minute," McGraw said. "Wait just a minute."

"We'll have to hide the hawk," Billy groaned. "Up the mountain farther—"

"Will you wait?" McGraw asked sharply.

"Yes, sir."

"They may not say a lot about the hawk. If they do, they have to say where the hawk is, isn't that right? And if they say where the hawk *is,* then don't they have to say what they were doing here?"

"They'll just lie about that part," Billy said.

"I don't know," McGraw replied. "Oh, I'll admit it looks bad. But it might not be. They might be ashamed—say nothing."

Billy stared at McGraw, trying to see if this was some strange kind of joke, but he saw that McGraw's face was wrinkled up the way it was when he was trying his hardest to puzzle through a difficult problem. Billy saw, then, almost instantly, something he had never known before. McGraw did not understand people in some of their aspects as well

192

as *he* did. Was it because he lived alone so much of the time, or were cause and effect reversed in this theory—did he live alone because of this failure to understand how people treated one another?

"They'll tell," Billy said. "They'll make it sound as bad as they can—for the hawk, and for you, too, probably."

"Billy's right," Jeremy said.

"Then you need to get down to your folks," McGraw replied. "You need to let people know what really happened."

"What if they don't believe us?" Jeremy asked.

"They will. They'll see that you two boys aren't liars."

It was just almost unbelievable! McGraw had a faith in people that made Billy feel a jaundiced old man. And yet, he saw, McGraw's suggestion was the only one that made any sense at all. Paw had to be told. Sheriff Sweeney had to know, too. Because whatever happened now, they might be involved as the law. Morrie and Robertson—and their friends—had to be prevented from coming back—for more of their 'fun' or for revenge.

"We'll git home," Billy decided. "We'll say what happened. We'll make sure we see what's going on. If there's any kind of bad reaction, one of us will git back up here and let you know."

McGraw nodded. "You sure you'll tell, Jeremy?"

Jeremy's Adam's apple went up and down. "No way to avoid it. I'll get a lickin', no question about that. But I'd rather tell Daddy—confess—than have him hear it from somebody else first."

McGraw took a deep breath. "Boys, I'm sorry you're in this mess."

"I guess it's too late to be sorry about it," Billy said. "Jeremy, we better git moving."

When Billy reached his house, the first thing he saw was

Sheriff Sweeney's pale brown mare in the front yard. Thinking it was a stroke of luck to have Sweeney at the house just when he needed to tell him about the incident on the mountain, Billy hurried inside. One look at Sweeney's face, and his father's, told him that the visit wasn't luck; the trouble had already reached town, and Sweeney was here because of it.

"Billy," his father said, "have you been up the mountain?"

"Yes, sir."

"With the—McGraw?"

"Yes, sir. I—"

"Suppose you tell us exactly what happened up there, then."

Billy gulped and told it as briefly and clearly as he could. The two men sat at the table over their coffee cups, glancing at each other now and then with expressions that grew grimmer as Billy's story unwound.

"It figures," Sweeney grunted when Billy concluded. "They tried to take the hawk?"

"Morrie picked him up, rough."

"And the hawk let him have it," Sweeney sighed. "Well, that no good—the punk asked for it, sounds like. But tell that to those people in town."

"We could do just that," Billy's father snapped. Then, as Sweeney looked blank, he added, "Take Billy and Jeremy to Springer, have them tell their story."

"I doubt Sled would let his kid go, Dan, and—"

"Billy, where is Jeremy?"

"He went home."

"—and even if Jeremy did go in, who says people would believe him or your boy, here, either?"

"You believe him," Dan Baker snapped.

"That's a little different." Sweeney tipped his hat back and brought his coffee mug to his lips, draining it. "See,"

194

he said, putting the mug on the table, "*I* know this isn't the first time Morrie and some of his buddies have been out, harassing folks. But do you figure anybody else is going to believe it? They'll say it's just an attempt to discredit Paul Carson as head of the vigilance committee."

"Why would we want to discredit Paul anyway?" Dan Baker asked disgustedly. "That doesn't even make sense!"

"It don't have to make sense," Sweeney said. "It didn't make sense when somebody went out and burned the Pruitt barn. Carson said the vigilantes didn't do it; Pruitt said *some* small band of riders did it, and put some lead into the house long enough to make sure he couldn't get out and douse the flames before they got going real good. But nobody believed Pruitt.

"It didn't make sense when that bunch of folks from the East, the McBrides, got shot at and scared out of their wits, and their wagon tore up, their very first night on their new claim, either. Paul Carson said it had to have been the bad element. But why would rowdies do stuff like that, when all it could do was stir up the vigilantes worse?"

Sweeney shook his head. "Morrie and his buddies probably did both deals—probably some others, too. They've been going around having the time of their lives, picking on people and raising Cain, and everybody has been blaming somebody else."

"Why would Morrie and those boys do such things?" Dan Baker asked.

"Maybe," Sweeney said bluntly, "because some people just are not worth two cents, and Morrie Carson is one of them."

"That's no good," Dan Baker said. "There's got to be a better explanation than that."

"Not for me. A bully is a bully. A bum is a bum. Morrie and some of them others are *both*—always have been, their daddies giving them everything, spoiling them rotten, protecting them whenever they do something bad."

Billy saw his father's face go slack with a startling new thought. "They might even have pulled some of the rough stuff in town that got the vigilante business stirred up in the first place."

"That just occurred to you, huh?"

"You thought about it before?"

"A long time ago."

"How is Carson acting now, about Morrie getting clawed?"

Sweeney considered the question. "Quiet. We talked. He says he don't believe Morrie's story. He wants to know what did happen. Most of all, though, he's scared of some of the others. There's hard feeling in that town."

Paw nodded. "Some of them will want to do something."

Billy blurted, "They wouldn't go after Mister McGraw!"

"A boy comes in, clawed by a hawk. The hawk is being kept by a crazy man, so-called. The town has a group that's already running off everyone who even looks a little different. It doesn't take any big leap of the imagination to guess what's next, Billy."

"But if Mister Carson doesn't tell 'em to—"

"Mister Carson isn't in charge anymore."

Sweeney said, "I want to take Billy and the Sled boy into town. Get them to tell their version."

"You think that will cool things off?"

"I don't know, but it can't hurt."

Paw frowned. "Are you willing, boy?"

Billy thought about it. He was scared. "Yes, sir," he said.

Paw nodded. "We'll go collect Jeremy, then."

They went outside, Billy following the two men. As she usually did when a male visitor came to talk business,

196

Billy's mother had gone off from the house; this time she was hoeing around the corn in the garden. Billy's father hurried out to the garden and leaned over the rickety fence to talk earnestly to her for a minute.

Sweeney told Billy, "Your daddy's been a big help to me, Billy."

"Yes, sir," Billy said, worried.

"Only two things have kept this from gettin' completely out of hand: my good luck in not having other stuff going on in the county, so I can stay right on top of this, plus your daddy's help. Having a local man on my side has made it a lot easier."

Wondering if it was going to remain easier, Billy said nothing. After another minute of conversation at the garden, his father walked to the barn and hauled out the saddle and gear, hurrying to catch and saddle the gray geld that had been his to use since the deputizing.

It took only a minute or two to have the horse ready, and Billy watched his father swing into the saddle with a grace and ease that betrayed that he had not always been a dirt farmer with only a plow horse to his name. His father brought the gray over easily and held down a hand. Billy sprang up and got on the horse's hindquarters behind his father.

"That's the Sled place just up there, right?" Sweeney said.

"Right."

The sheriff, his poor animal dwarfed by his huge size and weight, led the way. They cantered up the road, which the thin sun was fast drying after the morning rains. Off in the mountains, Billy noticed, were new clouds. By night-fall it was going to get bad again. He thought of McGraw up there alone, with the hawk, and felt a stronger pang of worry.

Sheriff Sweeney led the way across the sloping grassland

197

between the road and the dugout of the Sled family. Partway across the expanse, he slowed a bit and straightened in the stirrups, looking ahead. Billy peered around his father's body to see too.

The Sled family was out in front of the house, waiting: John Sled and his wife, Jeremy, and the other kids, ranging down to Joseph, who was a toddler.

"Why are they standing out like that?" Billy asked.

His father had stiffened in the saddle. "Waiting for us, maybe."

Sweeney led the way into the yard. The horses were reined up. John Sled, his face set grimly, looked up at them. "Git down if you like," he said.

Sweeney did not move. "We need Jeremy's help, John."

Sled nodded. "I thought that would be it."

"The boys need to tell their story in town—"

"The boy disobeyed me. Once can be a mistake. Twice or three times is more serious. He's staying right here."

"The mood in town was already bad. Now that other boy has been hurt, maybe pretty bad. Unless these two boys tell their side, and convince folks of it, some of those hotheads in there might try to take it out on the old man."

Sled did not blink. "No concern of mine."

"We're asking your help, John. It's serious."

"The boy stays here. He don't leave my sight. Later we're going to the woodshed. Then he's gonna have plenty of work to keep him busy. He won't be gallivantin' around for quite a spell."

"We'll take him. We'll have him back in an hour or two."

"No, sir."

"Mister McGraw might git hurt—" Jeremy began to plead.

"Shut your mouth, boy," Sled said.

Billy's father said, "I know how you feel, John. But if it might head off some violence—"

198

"He stays here," Sled said. "An' your boy, he stays at his place, as far as I'm concerned. If you git what I mean."

Sweeney's heavy hands rested on the horn of his saddle like chunks of meat, and his eyes were just as dead. "You won't help?"

"Nyawp."

Sweeney sat still a minute, then touched the brim of his hat. "Mrs. Sled." He turned his horse.

They rode away from the house. Billy could feel the tension in his father's body.

"You go on back home," Sweeney said bitterly.

"What will *you* do?" Paw asked.

"Go back to town. See what I can find out."

"Maybe there won't be any bad reaction," Paw said.

Sweeney spat soundlessly. "Most of the people in the vigilance group are good people pushed too far. Some ain't. There's hotheads. Some have mumbled against that old man on the mountain for a long time. And now the ball's been opened on killin' or anything else, ain't it."

"If some of them try to do anything to that man—"

"I'll stop 'em," Sweeney cut in, as if saying he would churn some butter, or cut some wood.

"Alone?"

"Maybe alone."

Billy's father sat straighter. "I'll help you, if I can."

Sweeney looked at him. "Mob action is like a sickness. If they get going, they don't stop easy."

"I know that. I know that better than you think."

"It's not really your fight."

Billy saw his father's rueful smile. "I've been dealt in."

Sweeney thought about it, then nodded. "Go home. I'll look into it. Keep your own look-see. I don't expect anybody would move on you, but there's no telling anymore."

"I'll be careful."

"And I'll let you know," Sweeney said.

They parted.

Billy went home with his father, and by the lingering silence and solemnity of the man, he knew the situation was potentially far worse than anything in his experience led him to expect. There was a short, quiet conference between the parents—an exchange of words that the turning of backs and lowering of voices declared private. Then Billy's mother returned to cleaning vegetables, and his father went outside, looked around at the land and the mountains, took a deep breath, seemed to shake himself, and walked down to the garden. He began hoeing, but not as if his heart was in it.

Billy went out and joined him, collecting the weeds as they were hoed out and piling them along the fence of the pet pen. The sun had begun to peep through swollen black clouds, and the humidity made it hot. He saw his father pause to mop a shirtsleeve across his forehead, feel the bandage there, and frown.

"You all right, Paw?" he asked anxiously.

"Sure, boy. Fine."

"You look kind of peaked."

"You do too, as a matter of fact. Why don't you go in and ask your mother to rustle you up a fried pie or something?"

"Well, I guess I'll just stay here with you."

His father smiled at him. "You're a good boy, do you know that?"

It unaccountably embarrassed Billy. "I shouldn't of done all that with the hawk."

"What's done is done. We've got more important things to worry about right now."

"What's going to happen now?"

"I don't know."

"They wouldn't really bother Mister McGraw, would they?"

"Some would, I'm afraid."

"But he hasn't *done* anything!"

"You don't have to do much for some people to fear you, son. Being a little different is enough—for some people."

Billy put some weeds by the fence. "I thought they had killed you in town, Paw!"

His father grinned slowly. "Takes a lot to kill an old cuss like me."

It struck Billy forcibly: the way his father stood there, grinning, bandaged, leaning on the hoe—some new glimpse into *what his father was*. It had to do with coming here to claim new land, and fighting it for survival. It had to do with a lot more. All of it went to a sudden knowledge of the kind of man this man—this father of his—might really be. Billy sucked in a sharp breath because the vision was not clear, and he was not sure of it.

Whether he would have said anything about it on this one time when he had a chance, he would never know.

Because his father turned and frowned into the distance, toward the road.

A man was coming on horseback. There was no mistaking the thick silhouette.

Billy's father put the hoe against the fence and started for the front yard.

Sweeney stood at the front of the house, one foot hiked up on the edge of the stoop. "The hawk deal was bad enough. Carson tried to calm folks down, but nobody would listen. Not the hotheads, anyway. They're convinced the old man is a menace. Mister Chafflin got going. Talking about old men being corrupters of little boys, sometimes."

"That's—disgusting!" Billy's mother, standing back a few steps, gasped. "How dare they—"

"I'm only telling the truth of what's going on," Sweeney said uncomfortably.

"But you said that wasn't the worst," Paw said.

"Something else came up. Couldn't have come at a worse time. Naturally. It seems like some of the good folks have been checking up on each other."

"I don't understand what you mean."

"Somebody—I think it's the town clerk, maybe—Greene —wrote some letters. I don't know who all he checked on. But he says one letter went to Washington. Remember Herman, that used to live on the other side of town? Got himself elected representative, ended up in Washington doing something, I don't know. Anyway, somebody wrote him. I saw the letter that came back just today. It's not good."

"Not good about what?" Paw demanded. "Or who?"

"McGraw."

"What would anybody in Washington know about—"

"His war record."

"What would that have to do with—"

"He was a deserter."

"No!"

Billy heard his own voice before realizing he had shouted the denial.

Sweeney looked at him, and the sheriff's face massed in deep wrinkles of fat. "It's true."

"I don't believe it!" Billy protested. "He's brave! He's a good guy! He's—"

"The letter covers it," Sweeney said, looking as if the taste of every word was foul in his mouth. "He was with our side—the Union—at Vicksburg. I don't know for sure whether that's where it took place or not. But he was listed as a deserter, and later they tried him."

202

Billy's father, his face perplexed, shook his head slowly. "The war is over and done with. Whatever he did or didn't do—"

"He did it," Sweeney cut in heavily. "I've just been up there to see him."

The pang cut through Billy's midsection.

Paw said, "He admitted it?"

"He wouldn't talk about it—said there was some truth in it, it was his business. That's all." Sweeney spat. "He's a tough old man, in his own way."

Paw took another of those deep breaths and glanced worriedly at Mom. "Even if it's true, that's no excuse for anybody in town to do anything."

"Ordinarily," Sweeney said, "right. But now, *anything* is an excuse."

"What do you think they're planning to do?"

A fly buzzed around and alighted on Sweeney's bare forearm, and he casually swiped at it with a pudgy hand, catching it. He held his arm out to the side and let the fly go. "They're going to run him off."

"We can't let them," Paw said.

"I can't get any help."

"I'm here."

"And you're the only one."

"There must be others!"

"Why would there be others now? There haven't been. Some of them have the bloodlust themselves. Some go along because they're scared of reprisals. Others—" Sweeney sighed. "Others just—won't."

"Well, we can't let them run that man off. I know how they'd do it. With guns, or torches."

Sweeney nodded. "Or both."

"And he could be killed."

"He could."

"What do you plan to do about it?"

Sweeney's face twisted in anger. "Stay up twenty-four hours a day, if I can. Be in six places at once, if I can. Back them off, if I can."

"I'll help you," Billy's father said after a slight pause.

"You've done enough, Dan."

"I said I'd help you. Don't give me a good chance to back out. I don't have a very long gut, and I may take you up on it."

Sweeney's eyes flared approval. "The west slope. Near the road. They'll do it at night, the way they always do. And probably tonight. I could give you some flares—you could watch—"

"I'll be there tonight."

"I'm going to ask Carson if he wants to help me keep watch in town. Not wearing a badge. And I know I'm asking a lot of him. But I think he really has turned around on all of this."

"He could be valuable."

"If that wasn't the case, I think I'd ask him anyway." Sweeney paused. "A man needs a chance to redeem himself."

"With himself, you mean."

Sweeney nodded.

Paw started patting his pockets for his pipe. "All right. Good. You can count on me, too—for as much help as I'm capable of giving."

"You've already helped more than anybody like me could expect. And I'm still not sure I know why you've done it."

"I'm crazy," Paw said, "that's why." And he smiled.

Thirteen

With the approach of nightfall, the first miserable drizzle returned. In the house, Billy watched his father solemnly put on the old slicker and check his rifle. His father wore his oldest clothes, all gray and thick, for warmth, and his sturdiest work boots. The night was getting cold out there already. The fire felt good.

Billy's mother, standing beside the fireplace, betrayed her worry in the ashen color of her face. "Don't forget the jar of coffee," she said.

"I won't," Dan Baker grunted. He summoned a faint smile for her. "It won't stay hot very long, but it still ought to taste good if I'm out there very long."

"How long will you be out there?"

"Hope I'm out there until morning. I'm going to stay until daylight, unless something happens. So hope, will you?"

She nodded. "I'll hope." Her smile was a failure.

"Paw?" Billy said.

"Yes, son?"

"Are you *sure* you won't let me go?"

"I'm sure."

"I could help."

"I know you could. But you stay here."

"Aw!"

His father picked up the brick-red cylinder off the table and held it in his fist. "I hope this flare works if I need it. It's supposed to shoot up in the air and then burst, like flares they used in the war. At least this waxed paper ought to keep it dry." He started rolling the cylinder in the heavy, yellowish paper.

"You got matches?" Billy asked.

His father patted a pants pocket. "Plenty."

Billy stood with his mother and watched as his father put the wrapped flare and the rifle under his slicker, pulled his hat down low over his face and neck, and went to the door. He turned to them. "Don't worry."

Billy's mother laughed a brief, barking laugh. "Of course not. What on earth would I *worry* about?"

Dan Baker's grim smile flashed. Then he opened the door, letting in a flurry of icy rain and mist with the wind that fluttered the fire. The door closed and he was gone.

Billy's mother stood still for a minute or two. Then she turned to the fire and stirred it with the poker, although the fire didn't need stirring. Then she went to the table and got her sewing basket and carried it to the rocker. She sat down and looked at Billy.

"He'll be all right," she said.

Billy, his tension almost more than he could handle, nodded and went to the loft ladder.

"Where are you going?" his mother asked.

"I thought I could see him down the road a piece from the little window."

She nodded silent assent.

Climbing into the low-roofed loft, he crawled over his sleeping pallet to get to the small window in the peak of the roof. Looking out through the drizzle-streaked glass, which was very wavy anyway, he couldn't see a thing but blackness. His breath made fog on the inside of the glass. Disappointed and discouraged, he rolled over to his pallet and lay looking up at the rafters, close enough that he could reach out and feel their rough texture.

Lying still, he could hear the hiss and sputter of the fire, the draw of it through the chimney that went up through the loft, the gentle creak of his mother's rocker, the fluttering of drizzle on the roof shakes, and the murmur of cold wind.

He was so worried about his father, and about McGraw and Sweeney, that he felt a bit sick at his stomach. It was so dumb of his paw not to let him help. There were various approaches up the mountain, and he knew them better than his father or practically anyone else. But as far as he was concerned, they worried about possible danger, he guessed, or getting a snotty nose from some rain. They didn't give him a chance.

Some time passed. He reviewed the day, which seemed two weeks long.

If there was any way, he decided, he would still go up the mountain and try to help Paw. The major problem was with his mother, and getting out of the house.

Of course, there was always the window. You *could* slide it open far enough to get out, and you *could* go down the side of the house all right.

The question was whether you could do it quietly enough to avoid detection.

Below, his mother stirred. "Billy?"

"Yes, ma'am?"

"Do you plan to come back down here tonight?"

"No, ma'am."

"All right. I'm going to turn the lantern down, then."

207

"You through sewing?"

"I can't—concentrate tonight. I'm just going to watch the fire for a while. Are you going to go to sleep soon?"

"Yes, ma'am, I guess so."

"Billy?"

"Uh-huh?"

"Don't worry, son."

"Yes, ma'am."

"Good night."

"Night."

He lay there in the quiet. His mother, judging by the sounds, rocked for a while, then moved about the large lower room nervously, being quiet, with no pattern to her actions. Later there was more rocking, and then she prepared for bed. The cords and boards of the big bed creaked and groaned as her light weight got into the bed.

Billy had not undressed. The whole question of going out the window, and after his father, was still undecided. The rain pattered steadily on the slanting roof a foot over his head. He knew, on the one hand, that he ought to obey and stay right where he was. He knew, on the other, that he couldn't sleep.

If he *were* going, he thought, he would have to put on his heavier boots. So just for practice he put them on and silently laced them up, sitting on his pallet.

And he would need his sweater, that was for sure, and an extra pair of pants right on over the others, if you could squirm into them in such close quarters—which you could.

Then you would need your jacket, and your hat, naturally.

He sat on his pallet in the dark, fully clothed—over-clothed so much that he felt like a mummy—and wrestled with himself about going. He ought to stay. He ought to

208

go. He ought to obey Paw. He ought to be where he could help.

Should. Shouldn't. Yes. No. Yes. No.

Finally, the welter of conflicting thoughts got so hot and heavy that he thought his brain was going to burst. In an instant—knowing this had probably been his decision all along, and he had just been postponing it—he crawled across the loft to the window again.

He slid it open cautiously, and the air and drizzle that swept in were cold.

But not half so cold as the rain and wind that began pelting gently, insistently, against him as he climbed down the side of the house with fingers already starting to go numb.

He knew where his father would be on the ridge line that guarded the approach to the mountain. There were only three or four spots where boulders were piled high enough on the slope to provide either cover from the weather or a good spot for observation of the road. So finding Paw, to help him, wasn't likely to be that hard.

It was not until Billy was slogging across the back meadow in the wet blackness, already soaked and shivering, that the *real* problem occurred to him: how to get Paw to accept his help—not send him packing down the mountain again with his fanny on fire.

After all, Paw had been fairly explicit in telling him to stay home. Billy had been so anxious to have a part in whatever might go on that he hadn't considered how unlikely it was that Paw would change his mind inside an hour or two.

It was a problem he should have started thinking about a lot sooner. The rain pelted down steadily, stinging coldly through the jacket, which didn't even strain the water, much less try to shed any of it. He was getting soaked and miserable, his shoes were heavy with slippery mud, there were wet burrs in his pants legs, and he couldn't see much through the black night. The storm was getting worse: The wind was beginning to pick up, hurling the rain in sheets. A vein of lightning splintered across the sky, making everything a vivid blue-white for a split second, and then it was dark again as the thunder clapped sharply.

There was just no way, however, that Billy figured he could think about turning back. McGraw might be in danger, and he knew his father stood an even better chance of being miserable and exposed right this minute.

He had to go try to help. His father, seeing his sincerity, probably would welcome him.

He struggled on up the hillside, and cross-country. The storm made it impossible to see the lights from Springer, below. Wind, gusting harshly, threw leaves and brush and trash against him, around him, and up into the black vacuum of the sky. He lost track of time. His teeth chattered, and under the wet clothes he was shaking all over. He knew where his place was, however, he kept telling himself: It was with Paw, where he could help McGraw—

"*Billy!*"

The voice was right next to his ear, shouting over the wind and startling him badly. Strong hands grabbed his shoulders, turning him, and he stared up into his father's gaunt, rain-streamered face. His father's hands were like steel bands on his arms.

"What are you doing out here?" Paw yelled on the wind.

"I came to help—" Billy began.

"You crazy kid!" Paw grabbed his arms differently and hauled him across the muddy road, toward some jumbled boulders on the higher ground side. The wind whipped at both of them, driving cold rain into Billy's skin like fiery

210

needles. He saw he had been so miserable that he had blundered right past the first place he had figured earlier as a likely spot for his father to be camped out—and his father had been there, all right, and on the alert.

Now, numbed, Billy allowed the tall man to lead him in among the big boulders along the slope. He barely saw the place between huge rocks where the wind whipped the edge of a canvas. His father shoved him between the rocks, raised an end of the canvas, and pushed him inside.

It felt warmer between the big rocks, and it was definitely a little drier. Boulders protected them from the wind on two sides, and at the back and front of the rocky grotto his father had lashed canvases. The one at the back took the brunt of the wind and rain, but was also tied full to both sides and over the top, making a tentlike roof. The canvas to the front, allowing a view outside, down the slope, and toward the road, was gaped about a foot, and allowed some sputtering rain and mist inside. The protected area was about six feet square, and although the ground was muddy from leaks, and the wind whistled right through once or twice in the first minute, it was like a fortress compared with what Billy had been in.

His father turned Billy to face him. Billy could scarcely make out his features. He looked grimly angry. "You should have stayed home, boy."

"I wanted to help, Paw!"

Dan Baker set his jaw. He seemed to be thinking hard about what to do next, possibly weighing the dangers and discomfort of sending Billy back through the storm to the house.

"I can help you keep watch!" Billy told him.

"I think it's better for you to stay here than get back out in that," his father told him. He opened his heavy coat and spread his arms. "Get inside here and try to get warm."

211

"I'll get you all wet."

"Will you do what you're told? Once?"

Billy obeyed. His father's body felt big and hard and warm. He was, Billy saw, soaked through too. But there was warmth inside the heavy coat, even though it was heavy with rain. Warmth—and security.

His father closed the coat around both of them, awkwardly forming a tent within the tent. He moved around to resume his position, squatting in the mud behind the front gap, which allowed a view of the black night where the road was. Lightning flickered, briefly illuminating a nightmare landscape. Billy shivered as warmth began to soak into him. His father said nothing and he said nothing, but he kept peering into the night, trying to penetrate the darkness. He wanted to help.

His father, he thought, was the brave man he had always —until this had begun—assumed. There could be no doubt of it now, and part of the proof was in the way they were here together in the wet night, ready to face whatever came. The knowledge was enormously comforting.

Nevertheless, an odd formality surrounded them as his father poured some of the coffee from the jar and offered it to him. The coffee was already cold, but it tasted good. Billy said his thank you very carefully as he handed back the tin cup.

He knew what his father was made of now, he thought, and he was proud. But the formality showed that some things could not be said—some thoughts not entertained— without doing harm. Their relationship had been damaged. He felt a great sadness. Could something as fragile as this ever be repaired? Was love like a fine piece of glass, which, once broken, could not be made as it was again no matter how strenuous the effort?

It was a terrible thought, perhaps the worst he had ever

212

encountered. He strained his eyes at the night, telling himself that all a person could do was *try*.

He would try, he told himself. He would go on trying as long as he lived. And right now, the way to try was to help —to watch the night with this man, and stay close to him. He huddled closer.

Time passed. The misting rain thrummed on the canvas. Billy's eyes grew sticky, and his eyelids became heavy. He fought exhaustion. It wouldn't hurt, he thought, to rest his eyes just a minute.

He drifted.

He slept—perhaps a moment, perhaps an hour—and then awoke with a start.

They were coming.

It was almost dawn—the sky had that pearly sheen in the east that said the sun was on the way—and the view from the tent was restricted, yet adequate to tell him everything.

He had been awakened, he imagined, by the stiffening of his father's body in alarm. Now his father was leaning to the far side of the hiding place, getting the wax-papered package that contained the flare. Water dropped off the edges of the tent, and the ground beneath them was soggier than it had been earlier in the night. From wispy, fast-moving clouds overhead, only a steady, light drizzle fell.

Billy saw all this in a second, however, because his attention was immediately seized by the movement and illumination down the hill, slightly to the left, about three hundred yards distant in the darkness.

There were horsemen there. He couldn't tell how many, but one of them had a small, brightly smoking torch going. It gave little light except straight down toward the ground, and Billy saw, leaning closer to the front flap, that the man carrying the torch had fashioned some kind of shield to go around it. Some light was probably necessary; the brush and rocks on the hillside were treacherous, gleaming under rivulets of water, and the horses were laboring.

Hurrying, Billy's father unwrapped the flare, which had a wooden tail and some fins that would act just like a rocket once the wick had been lighted. Pressing the fuse out straight, Paw stuck the end of the firework into the soggy ground just outside the opening of the tent. He got into his pockets for matches, found some, gave Billy a warning look, and cracked the match head on the rock.

The match didn't light.

Frowning, Paw whipped the match head over the rock again. It left a long red streak on the boulder, but didn't even spark.

On the third try, the match broke. Paw tried another— and another—with identical results. Despite the chill pre-dawn wind, sweat stood out on his face. He rummaged through his pockets and tried some matches from a different pocket with the same lack of results.

Watching, Billy saw that he had been careful to protect the flare. It looked perfectly dry and well preserved. But he had forgotten to take equal care of the matches. They had soaked all night in his wet pants pockets, and would not begin to light.

"It's not going to work," Paw muttered, hurling a match from him.

Down the hill, the horsemen were moving in a line that paralleled the road, but stayed below it. They had moved a little nearer and a few hundred feet higher. Far below them, the faintest suggestion of a handful of town lights shone through the misting rain.

"Maybe," Billy whispered, "they ain't vigilantes."

"What else would they be?"

"Maybe they ain't going after Mister McGraw."

"What else is up here?"

Billy couldn't argue with either point. Crawling out of his father's heavy coat, he discovered that he was still soaked all the way through. His joints throbbed. He felt unmistakably feverish. But none of this mattered very much. The riders below, moving along at a slow pace, were clearly moving higher. They would pass near this spot, and their path could lead to only one place: McGraw's.

"I don't see any sign of Sweeney," Billy's father said, peering through the hole in the canvas. "These must have gotten away without him seeing them. If I could make the blasted flare work!"

"I could run for town," Billy suggested.

"By the time you could get there, it would be all over."

The simple statement, rather than the ritual concern over his safety, shocked Billy more than anything else could have. His father didn't want him to go to town because it would be a futile gesture: *McGraw didn't have that much time left.*

"Are you going to try some more matches?" Billy asked.

"They're gone."

Below them, the horsemen came along in the darkness, now about two hundred yards distant. Billy watched his father's face harden in thought and desperation.

"What are you going to do?" Billy asked.

"Stop them. Right here."

"How?"

"It looks like there are five or six of them. We're hidden here. I'll let them get up onto the road surface. Then I'll call to them and identify myself and order them to turn back. They won't be able to see me. They won't know how many of us there are."

It sounded like a desperate gamble, but Billy accepted

215

it immediately. "If you've got an extra gun, Paw, I can shinny around to another place—"

"No, you've got something more important to do, now."

A pulse thumped in Billy's neck, paining him. "Yes, sir?"

His father glanced to the rear. "Get up there. Let McGraw know."

"And leave *you?* No, sir! I—"

His father grabbed his arm so roughly and so hard that he almost yelled. "Boy, don't argue with me now! Our job is to save that man's hide, if we can. *Your* part of that job is to get up there and warn him."

"What happens to *you?*"

"Why, boy, probably nothing. I'll probably bluff them right out of it here in a few minutes."

"Then why should I have to go warn—"

"Billy, *will you do what you're told?*"

Billy stared into his father's face. He saw the strained muscles and the look in the eyes. He understood that he *had to* obey.

"Yes, sir," he said.

His father nodded and took another glance out the front canvas. The riders were moving very slowly, perhaps because of the difficult, wet terrain, or perhaps to time their arrival at some point with the break of dawn light. They did not seem a lot closer than before.

"Boy, if all's quiet down here, you just keep McGraw alerted, right? And you stay there and wait for me, because I'll get up there as soon as the coast is clear."

"Yes, sir."

"If you hear shooting, on the other hand, that means they're not turning back for me. In that case, you'd better make it clear to McGraw that he'd better get clear of this place for right now, until we can get things straightened out."

216

"If I hear shooting! Paw, that'd mean they was fighting you!"

"Not necessarily," his father said with that soft, ironic smile. "They start giving me a bad time, I'll shoot a couple rounds into the sky, hoping the noise will carry all the way down to town." He looked at Billy and seemed to see that he wasn't quite buying it. "They might shoot at *me,* too, of course, just to try to scare me off, put me in my place, get by me easy. But they're not going to try to hurt me, son. You *know* that. I'm the real law around here."

Billy's teeth chattered again, and this time it was not from the cold alone. "Are you sure *they* know that?"

Paw grinned. "You'd better git. Can you climb out the back way, there?"

"Yes, sir."

"Okay, then. Good luck, boy."

Billy looked at him and hesitated. In the still air, with the drizzle almost gone, the distant sound of horsemen carried to the tent now: creaking leather, the jingle of spurs and clopping of hooves in mud and on rock. Billy felt a stab of fear for his father and the need to say something— he didn't quite know what it was.

"Paw," he said thickly, "I—"

His father's face set. "I know, boy. Now will you *git?*" He reached out and caught Billy startlingly close in an instant's bearhug. When he pushed Billy back, his eyes looked bright. "Go," he said.

Billy crawled to the back of the makeshift tent, raised the canvas, and crawled out on his belly. He was already so mud-soaked and cold again that it hardly registered on his senses. He squatted low, looking around to make sure he had his bearings, then moved up through the rocks, staying below their tops.

By the time he had moved a hundred feet, he glanced

217

back and could no longer pick out which set of boulders was covered by canvas—had been his home this night, and still sheltered his father. The pink steam of the horsemen's torch shone below in darkness. The sky to the east was a grayer pearl now, touched near the horizon by the faintest bands of pink. Light was very near.

Turning, he scrambled up through more rocks.

"Mister McGraw! Mister McGraw!"

First dawn light etched the face of the cliff. As Billy reeled into the clearing, the door of the cabin burst open in response to his shout. The old man, half-dressed, came to meet him.

"What's happening, sonny? You're out of breath! You're—"

Billy gasped for air. "They're coming after you! My paw is down there, trying to hold them off, but you got to git out of here—"

McGraw's arms enclosed him, engulfing him in the odors of tobacco and woodsmoke and strong, masculine sweat. "Take it easy, Billy. Take it easy, son. Tell me what's going on. Take it one step at a time."

Billy struggled to tell it as clearly and straightforwardly as possible. He hurried his words, and McGraw, his face growing harder, listened in silence.

"Your daddy is still down there, then?" he asked finally.

"If he's all right he is!"

McGraw started to turn away. "I'd better be getting down there to see."

"No!"

"Don't you want your own father helped, boy?"

"Paw wanted you *warned*. That's why he took the chance, don't you see? If you go down there now, you're just messing things up worse!"

218

McGraw looked somber. "What is it I should do, then?"

"Run."

"That don't set right, youngster."

"If you stay here, they'll burn your place. They might do more than that."

McGraw's eyes narrowed. "More?"

"They might—hurt you."

The older man heaved a sigh and looked off into the distance, a distance of time as well as space. "A man gets tired of moving on."

"But we're trying to *save* you!"

McGraw returned his gaze to Billy's face and smiled briefly. "Yes." He reached out and tousled Billy's rain-soaked hair. "I guess you and your daddy have gone to a right lot of trouble to try to save me, haven't you."

"You'd better *run.*"

"Yes, I guess that's right. They'll come—if not today, then tonight or tomorrow—keep trying until they either succeed in getting to me, or hurt or kill someone else—"

"I can help you git ready," Billy told him. "Maybe you'll just have to hide a few days, and then—"

"No," McGraw said firmly. "I'm going to leave for good, boy."

"But things will settle down—it'll be okay—"

"No. You can't leave a place and be gone, and then go back. It isn't the same. When a man moves—he has to move."

Billy stared at him, not fully comprehending, but seeing that this meant he would never see McGraw again.

McGraw said, "You'll have to take care of your own hawk, too, of course."

"I can't," Billy said, surprising himself with how certain this knowledge had been within him all this time.

"Of course you can," McGraw said. "You've finished the training. He's ready to fly free. You can keep him at your house."

"No." Tears blurred Billy's vision.

"Your daddy will let you."

"Maybe he would. But somebody would just have to shoot that ole hawk down in the valley. They'd have to shoot him because he hurt Morrie, or just because he's big and fine and strong and flies around, free. Somebody would have to *git* him, down there."

McGraw stared at him for a minute.

"You'd better hurry," Billy told him.

McGraw went quickly into his house in the cliff.

Walking across the yard, Billy went to the hawk shed. He took the glove off the nail outside, put it on, and went into the shed.

Inside it was dark, and smelled strongly of the acrid odor of the hawk's eliminations during the night. But it was a sharply *alive* stench, not unpleasant. The hawk stirred on its perch.

Moving slowly, as he always did around the hawk, Billy knelt beside it. "Okay, you ole dummy," he murmured. "It's jus' me. I'm takin' you outside, see? Nothing to worry about. This is a big day for you. Come on, now."

He held out his arm and the hawk obediently stepped up onto the glove.

Outside, the drizzle had finally ended. Clouds hung low, swollen, over the tops of the mountains. The hawk turned its head sharply, pivoting about to see this cooler, wetter world. Its talons gripped Billy's arm through the glove with familiar tension.

"I guess you feel like flying *some*, anyhow," Billy said thickly. "Course you've got pretty lazy, pretty no-'count."

McGraw appeared in the doorway of his house. He had a

220

single burlap sack tossed over his shoulder. It bulged with the few possessions he had decided to take with him. He saw Billy and the hawk, and walked over to them. He stroked the hawk's breast with the back of his index finger.

"S'posed to use the feather, of course, but I s'pose it don't hurt once in a while."

"Is that stuff all you're taking?" Billy asked.

"That's all."

"Will you hide, or are you really going?"

"I'm going, Billy boy."

"For good?"

"For good."

"I want to—thank you for all the help you've given me with the hawk."

"That's all right, sonny. I enjoyed it."

Billy took a breath. "Only—I'm going to turn this hawk loose."

"You don't have to do that, youngster!"

"No, like I said: They'd shoot him down there. I can't make him hide all the time. And right now my daddy—see, I don't know where Paw *is*, actually, or if he's even alive, and he didn't want me to have no hawk—" Billy broke down and sobbed.

McGraw put a heavy arm around him. "Aw, sonny—"

"I'm okay," Billy insisted, shrugging him off. "You better git going, now, though, because you've messed around a long time. And I've got to let this dumb ole hawk loose before somebody maybe gets here and tries to hurt him."

Solemnly, McGraw backed away from him and watched.

Still having trouble with blurred vision, Billy unwound the swivel line from his hand and gently slipped the jesses down low on the hawk's feet so they would drop free when the bird took flight. Without thinking about it, Billy reached his free hand into his pocket to check for the small, wooden whistle. It was there, but then he realized that he didn't need it anymore.

"You have a nice life, you ole dummy, you hear?"

The hawk stared at him, unblinking.

Billy lowered his arm. The hawk stirred. Billy tossed. The hawk leaped into the air.

Its wings working strenuously, the large bird remained low to the ground for about twenty feet, heading directly for the brush, as it often did on the tether line. But as if remembering the work recently with the swinging lure, it swung upward, turning, almost going upside down as it swooped back toward the spot where Billy stood. It came low past him in a rush, as if looking for the lure, swung on past, rose high again in a beautiful turn, and came back a second time. Its eyes, as it shot by, watched Billy with a bright intensity.

"Go on, go on!" Billy yelled. "You ain't tied, you dummy!"

The hawk pivoted overhead, came down the chute, and landed midway between Billy's position and McGraw's.

"He sure wants to work the lure," McGraw said.

"Well, he won't!" Billy said. "Not any more! He's so dumb, he's free and he doesn't even know it!"

"He's not dumb, sonny. He's trained. Well."

"Go *on*, hawk!" Billy yelled, kicking dirt in the hawk's direction.

McGraw shuffled over. "I dunno about the hawk, youngster, but I'm on *my* way."

Billy was so busy being tough, he merely sniffled and frowned up at the older man. "Better be careful."

"I will," McGraw promised.

"And you'll write me?"

"Well, maybe I will, anyway."

"I'm—much obliged for everything, Mister McGraw."

222

McGraw smiled and turned. He walked past his shed and his house without another glance, and went into the brush beside the cliff. In a moment he reappeared, working his way up through the rocks. He would, Billy saw, reach the top of the cliff within a few minutes by this route, and then he would be gone.

The hawk fluttered its wing nervously and walked around.

"You better fly!" Billy told it. "You better git away, in case folks come after you!"

The hawk looked at him. There was so much intelligence in those keen eyes, it was heartbreaking. The hawk *knew*, Billy thought. It did not understand, but it knew something very unusual was taking place, and it was looking to him for a signal of what it should do next. It hurt to see the dumb old thing sitting there, *depending* on him that way. The hawk was so beautiful, it had flown so perfectly.

The hawk moved around nervously, waiting to be picked up.

Billy scooped up a small rock and hurled it. "Go on! Go *away!*"

The hawk took to the air in alarm. Its wings working strongly, it rose higher this time—higher than it had ever flown in its life, rising almost vertically with powerful wing strokes over the trees. Then it turned and swooped, turning, looking down at Billy again.

Out of the brush and woods below his position, Billy saw another movement, which drew his attention momentarily from the hawk. It was his father, hatless, his clothing soaked from tearing through the wet brush.

"I turned them back," he said with tired satisfaction. "But I'm afraid they'll return after a while. They only backed down because I surprised them."

"It's all right, Paw. Mister McGraw is gone."

"Gone?" Paw's face wrinkled.

"He's left. For good." Billy pointed to the top of the cliff, where the land line moved across toward the edge of the mountain saddle. "There."

His father shaded his eyes with a cupped hand to look, and as he did so, McGraw moved into view, high up there, against the sky, striding fast. He moved along the saddle line in silhouette.

The hawk wheeled through the wispy-clouded sky above McGraw's position, balanced on the strength of its broad wings, a streak of speed charcoaled against gray.

"That's not your hawk, is it?" Paw asked, surprised.

"No, sir," Billy choked. "Not now, it isn't."

Paw's face showed he understood. "I'm sorry, boy."

"I am too, Paw." Then he added in a burst, "I *doubted* you."

"We all have doubts. They're part of living—of growing up."

"I'll never doubt you *again!*"

And with these words the tears did come, finally, and he fiercely hugged his father's waist. "I love you, Paw! I'm sorry! I'm *sorry!*"

His father's big arms closed tightly around him. "It's okay, Billy. It's okay, son."

Billy sobbed with hurt and regret and relief. McGraw vanished over the ridge. The hawk swung once through a broad orbit of the sky, circling, uncertain, lost. Then it, too, went out of sight beyond the line of rocks. Billy clung to his father.

It was over.

Fourteen

William R. Baker, attorney-at-law, had gone to sleep very late, kept awake by the flood of old memories, and he awoke early, the memories still strong in his mind.

Dressing, he packed his suitcase carefully, because he would be concluding the land talks today, and heading back toward Colorado. It struck him that in some ways it seemed like much more than a dozen years since that morning on the side of the mountain overlooking the little town of Springer. And yet how often he remembered all of it, vividly, as he had last night and this morning.

He had never seen McGraw again. The vigilantes had done their job, burning his sheds and house the same afternoon. But in the process one of the vigilantes was accidentally burned, badly, on the face. After that, there was an inevitable reaction to the outburst of violence. The reaction got a mighty shove when Robertson, Morrie Carson's companion, had too much to drink and told the truth about the hawk's attack—telling all of it in a crowded saloon that became deathly still as Robertson babbled the tale, unaware that people had stopped laughing with him at the absurdity of the sequence of incidents—unaware, that is, until it was much too late. Following this incident, Sweeney's re-election had been easy, a new, regular deputy had been named, things had begun to settle down.

Billy, though, had not forgotten. The loss of both McGraw and the hawk haunted him. He still thought of it often, when he knew it should be long behind him and forgotten.

He was still thinking about it when he met Chumley, the land group's representative, in the lobby of the rooming house to go to breakfast.

"Say," Chumley grinned at him. "You must be more worried about *some* part of this deal than you let on!"

"Why do you say that?" Baker asked.

"You look a little peaked, like you didn't get too much sleep last night."

Baker smiled, and, as he walked to the cafe with Chumley and ate breakfast, he told the other man a few of the details of the old story.

"Real odd!" Chumley said. "And you never ran into this old man again?"

"I've been in a hundred towns west of Denver since I began law practice," Baker admitted. "And each time it's crossed my mind that the more I travel, the more likely it is that one day I'll run into word of him again. But I never have. And I suppose he'd be too old now. I suppose he's dead, like the hawk."

Chumley nodded solemnly. "Yes, sir, that's true. And I started to say—but no, that'd be too wild, too much coincidence—"

"Started to say what?" Baker asked.

"Well, believe it or not, we've got *us* a crazy man of the mountain here, now, just like you did back there a long time ago."

"An old man?" Baker asked.

226

"Well, mighty hard to say. He's got a gray beard. He lives up there on that slope. See through the window where I'm pointing? No, to the left. There. Right. Takes a couple hours to ride up there. Stays to himself, he does. Nobody bothers him, he don't bother nobody. But—" Chumley paused and looked startled. "It would be too much to *ask*, that he'd be *your* mountain man—right?"

It *would* be too much to ask, too improbable. But within thirty minutes Baker had rented a horse and was on his way into the timber country, going the circuitous route up the mountain.

He felt strung tight and eager as he rode, although he knew the odds were a thousand to one against him. He had made other rides out of other towns in recent years to see mountain men: near Raton, in Oregon, once, on two occasions not far from Denver itself, once a few months ago in Wyoming. His specialization in land management and purchasing had already made him a traveler. He had already had his share of disappointments, looking for McGraw.

Still he rode higher. It felt good to be alone in the woods on horseback, and the two-hour time period that Chumley had estimated for the trip up seemed to pass quickly.

Ahead, through the high virgin timber, Baker spied a wisp of woodsmoke. He rode for it, letting the horse pick its own leisurely pace through woods, across beds of pine needles, down a gentle slope in the earth, a pause in the mountain's steady rise toward a snowy peak thousands of feet still overhead.

Then he came out onto a shelf and saw, just ahead, in a clearing, a log cabin with two small outbuildings. It was a poor place, but kept up so neatly that it looked like more than it was. He saw no sign of anyone in the area.

227

Riding up to the cabin, Baker dismounted. The wind sighed in the pines.

"Hello!" he called. "Anyone home?"

For a moment there was nothing. Then the door of the cabin swung open.

The man who stood there had a gray beard and long, straight gray hair. His shoulders slumped a bit, and there was a pot belly. He wore heavy gray pants and a red flannel shirt, and there was absolutely no question about it.

"McGraw!" Baker burst out incredulously.

The old man squinted at him. "What? Who are you? What do you want?"

"I'm—Billy," Baker said, struggling for the best way to make himself remembered. "Billy Baker. I knew you in Springer, Colorado. You lived on the mountain, and I brought you a hawk—"

"*Billy?*" McGraw gasped. And then, before Baker could react, McGraw straightened up and strode with the stride of a young man across the front yard of the cabin. He grabbed Baker in his arms and they embraced.

Later, after the first burst of incredulous questions on both sides, McGraw invited Baker into the cabin for coffee. It was an immaculate little place, and the coffee was even better than Baker remembered it when once he had had that instead of cocoa with McGraw's cookies.

"I can't get over it," he told the old man with a grin. "I had really given up ever finding you!"

"What brings you here?" McGraw asked.

Baker told him about his law degree and his work and the land deal pending here. Then impulsively he told McGraw how the vigilantes had burned the cliffhouse, and what had happened afterward.

228

McGraw nodded, his face a thousand happy wrinkles. "And your daddy? Is he still alive, then, and well?"

"He died four years ago."

"I'm sorry to hear that, Billy—or perhaps I should call you 'William' now, or even 'Mister Baker.' Eh?"

" 'Billy' is good, and you know it, sir."

"Your mother? Is she still alive?"

"Yes, she lives in Denver now, with my younger sister. The two of them are together, I mean; my sis is only ten now."

McGraw nodded. "Having such a younger child; it gives your mother something to live for."

"Yes," Baker agreed.

Leaning forward on the table, McGraw narrowed his eyes. "There was another lad. I can't recollect his name, but he came with you once or twice. He brought a hawk of his own once, but it was a poor thing and very sick—"

"Jeremy," Baker supplied. "Jeremy Sled."

"Yes! The same! Tell me: Whatever became of him?"

"He still lives near Springer. He has his own farm now. He's married, has a wife and four children—"

"Four!"

"The last I heard," Baker said with a grin. "There might be five by now."

"Is that a fact!"

"But what about you, sir? How have you made it? What happened to you when you left Springer? How have the years treated you?"

"I came here, believe it or not, and had this very place built within a few months after I had left Colorado."

"And you've stayed here ever since?"

McGraw smiled. "Times are changing, a little. People don't think an old man is crazy just because he wants to live alone on a mountain. People leave me alone, and I leave them alone, except for now and again, some boy comes around, asking me to help mend a rabbit's broken leg or a bird's wing."

"You still work with wild creatures, then," Baker smiled.

"Indeed, sir, yes. I always did, you know. That was why I was a scout back in the war—maybe why that thing happened that let some people think I was a traitor."

Baker looked at the old man, and said nothing.

"You heard those stories," McGraw said.

"Right at the end—someone said something."

McGraw nodded sadly. "Of course they would, since they were wanting to justify getting rid of me."

Baker drained his coffee cup. He wanted to ask about it, but couldn't. The old sense of loyalty to McGraw was back as strongly as if he were still a little boy.

McGraw cleared his throat and said, "It happened at Arkansas Post, you know."

Baker leaned back and the old man told it.

He had been a scout for forces under General McClernand. General Grant, moving toward Vicksburg, had been having difficulty making headway, and had sent orders to McClernand to open a siege of Vicksburg without delay. McClernand, moving south down the river, could have obeyed. But he had political ambition, and wanted a spectacular victory on his record. Instead of moving southeast toward Vicksburg, he turned his forces northwest, into Arkansas, and hit Arkansas Post.

The fort surrendered after sharp fighting, but Grant, when he heard about it, was furious. He ordered McClernand and his forces back to Vicksburg.

Unfortunately for McGraw, his group of scouts had already been captured before the withdrawal orders arrived. He and his five other scouts had surrendered during the fight rather than being mowed down after they were cut off

230

from the main force of attacking troops. Paroled a few days later, McGraw and his men had rejoined their outfit. But in the bitterness and recriminations over McClernand's unauthorized side trip, a routine enquiry into failure to answer a muster call while they were prisoners had almost turned into a hanging trial for McGraw and his men. Finally they had been acquitted, but not before the charges went into the record, a permanent blot that the eventual acquittal could not erase.

"It followed you a long time, that record," Baker mused.

"Indeed it did," McGraw agreed.

"You're not bitter?"

"Why be bitter? It's done now, and gone."

"And you still work with boys and wild things. I think I would have ended up too bitter—too closed-in."

McGraw's eyes danced. "Remember that hawk of yours?"

"Every day," Baker admitted. "If there's anything I'll ever regret, I guess it's that—somehow—I didn't keep that bird, or at least get to see him work."

"It took courage to release him the way you did. You did it to save his life."

"I don't know if it worked, though," Baker admitted. "I never saw a trace of him again."

"I'm not surprised at that."

Baker looked at him.

McGraw said slowly, "The hawk followed me. It didn't seem to know what to make of everything. It followed me all that day—kept landing near me, as if he was begging. So I finally took pity on the poor, dumb thing, and took him in."

Baker was delighted. "You mean you took the hawk along?"

"That I did, sir!"

231

Baker thought about it. "I'm glad it didn't die in the wild," he admitted after a while.

"It certainly didn't do that," McGraw chuckled.

"What did finally happen to it?"

"Well, hawks live a long time, you know. Fifteen or twenty years." McGraw paused and watched Baker with lively eyes.

Puzzled, Baker didn't know what to say. "I don't get what you're driving at."

McGraw heaved himself out of the chair and walked briskly to the door, pulling it open. "Come on."

Following the old man outside and around the cabin, Baker had the fleeting suspicion that the hawk might be— could somehow—but he knew that *was* impossible. Was he going to see a grave? McGraw was a sentimental old fool, just as he was a sentimental young one.

They reached the back of the cabin. There was a small cleared area. There was a perch on the ground. On the perch was a hawk. It looked the same. It sat on the perch the same. It was heavier, but it *did* look the same. Baker's mind reeled.

"He's old and cranky now," McGraw chuckled, "but he still works every day."

Unable to believe the pleasure detonating through his mind and memory, Baker stood rooted, staring. The hawk was regal, ignoring him.

"Would you like to fly him, then?" McGraw asked, reaching for a glove that hung on a nail.

"I don't know—if I could," Baker admitted huskily. "I haven't worked another hawk, I—"

"I think he'll work for you," McGraw said with a smile. "Here, now, I'll toss and you can call and catch. I'll just find the whistle for you."

"You don't have to do that," Baker said, and he reached

232

93972

into his coat pocket. He took out the whistle he had carried ever since that morning.

"So you saved that, did you!" The old man said softly.

"I did."

McGraw chuckled and walked to the perch. Bending low, he let the hawk step up onto his gloved arm. The hawk was very alert, yet very calm. He was watching Baker now, but showed no alarm. Baker pulled his glove on, a tumultuous gladness within him. It was his hawk. There was no doubt. They knew each other still. No one would have believed that, he thought. But he knew it.

McGraw, beaming, walked out to the center of the clearing, the hawk riding easily on his arm. Baker moved across the clearing, the whistle ready to call, his own glove in place for the hawk to come to him and land. The thin sunlight poured down on him, and he was sweating with joy and nervousness and a feeling that a dozen years had never been, and he was a boy again, but this time *completed*.

McGraw poised with the fine, strong, beautiful hawk.

"Are you ready, then?"

"Yes!"